Emily's Dreams

Serendipity, Indiana - Book Two

by

Magdalena Scott

Emily's Dreams

Edited by Karen Block

Trade Paperback Release: August 2015
ISBN10:   0-9862118-3-4
ISBN13:   978-0-9862118-3-6

Digital Release: August 2015
ISBN-10:   0-9862118-2-6
ISBN-13:   978-0-9862118-2-9

Cover Design by Calliope-Designs.com
Stock Art by www.thinkstockphotos.com

DEDICATION AND ACKNOWLDGEMENTS

Emily's Dreams is dedicated to Theresa Zink
whose friendship has been, and continues to be,
an undeserved gift.

She also gets huge thanks as
Theresa Zink, MS, PT
for reading this story and taking the time
to help me make Emily's
injuries and rehabilitation plausible.

Theresa - Emily and I appreciate you!

Chapter One

Turn the page, Emily.

There it was again—the same disembodied voice I'd heard countless times, giving me the same inexplicable direction. If I could find a page to turn, literally or figuratively, maybe the voice would stop nagging me. Maybe, too, I'd finally know what direction my life was supposed to take. Considering my lack of focus in the past, there was almost unlimited opportunity for improvement.

I opened my eyes. The tiny room I inhabited now in my parents' home was painted marshmallow-crème white, and except for the bed and an antique dresser on the opposite wall, nearly bare.

I groaned as I pushed myself to a sitting position on the bed and managed to get both legs over the side of the mattress. My flannel gown had ridden up as I tossed in my sleep, so my knees were visible. The right one was still swollen, and I massaged my thigh.

"Come on. You're supposed to be getting better every day, remember? That was our deal." Truth be told, the leg hadn't been consulted, but the rest of me had decided it was in the best interest of all concerned.

Stretching to reach a shelf just above the bed, I unplugged my phone and replied to texts from my friends Karly and Danielle. I read a long email sent in the middle of the night by my brother, "the perfect child," Ben who felt guilty for not calling more often. Lucky Ben, at college getting an education and having the time of his life. He was on the right path to leave boring old Serendipity, Indiana, behind him.

I smiled, remembering what a pest he'd been as a little kid. Now that he was big and strong and generally pleasant, I seldom saw or heard from him. However, I was in frequent contact with the twins, our seventeen-year-old sisters who seemed bent on driving all of us completely bonkers. The faces of Hannah and Taylor flashed into my mind and I groaned again.

Setting my phone aside, I pulled Lightning off its perch at the head of the bed and hoisted myself up, bound for the bathroom. The fam said I was moving faster these days, but when you're twenty-five years old and dependent on an aluminum cane, it's hard to feel super positive about yourself. And yes, I named my cane. Doesn't everyone?

The bathroom mirror confirmed the scar along my jawline was still quite obvious, continuing to hinder nonexistent beauty pageant options. I washed my face, ran my fingers through my hair, and sighed at the dark circles that were still under my eyes.

But I'm getting ahead of myself. None of this will make sense to you if you don't know what happened before.

Just a heads-up, Taylor and Hannah won't be the only unpleasant types in this story. I'm sorry to say they learned a lot of attitude from their big sister—me.

First I need to tell you about the dream. Although it only happened once, it was emblazoned on my memory. But the voice telling me to turn the page…I'm not sure how many times I'd heard that. You'll have that little phrase memorized before long, I bet.

Chapter Two

Eyes tightly shut against the brightness of the sun, I lift my face to its warmth. Soothing heat bathes the skin of my neck and arms. A gentle breeze musses my blond hair, and soft tendrils tickle my neck. I slowly open my eyes and watch the breeze rustling the full skirt of my pretty blue dress. Surrounding the blanket I am sitting on, wild daisies sway and dance. The field of flowers extends as far as I can see, even from my vantage point high on the hill. Songbirds call as they chase each other across the sky.

Turn the page, Emily.

I didn't recognize the soft voice.

And what page?

I opened my eyes. The hill, the daisies, and my pretty blue dress were all gone. The movement of the breeze was gone. I also had the jarring recollection that my hair wasn't blond at all, but dark brown. Instead of that lovely scene, there was a very beige room, an assortment of medical equipment beeping and whirring, and the smell of disinfectant. The world's ugliest abstract-print curtain hung from a metal track in the ceiling.

So it had been a dream—but it had seemed, and felt, so real. I squeezed my eyes closed to block out the current view and try to recapture the place I'd just left.

"Dr. Waverly. Dr. D. L. Waverly." The intercom voice sounded bored. "Please call one nine."

I opened my eyes again and saw my mother sitting beside me, her head resting on one palm.

"Mom?" I whispered, in case she was asleep.

She was suddenly sitting straight up, on high alert. "Emily. You're awake! Oh, sweetie. We were so afraid…." Her hug was gentle but awkward because of the mass of tubes.

"What happened?" I choked out the words, and my throat hurt from the effort. Due to my rasping, it took Mom a moment to understand what I had said.

"You're in the hospital, sweetie. You had a car wreck about a week ago. Late at night, on your way home from an evening with your friends."

"Adam?"

"Adam was here to see you." Her voice was flat. "But he had to leave."

"Oh." So he was okay, at least. I knew she didn't like Adam any more than she had liked my previous boyfriends, and I had no desire to go down that road now. As long as he was fine, I knew I'd see him soon.

I didn't remember a wreck or what had led up to it. "Mom, was anybody else...?" Oh please, let nobody else be hurt—or worse.

She shook her head no. "Just you," she whispered. Her eyes filled with tears, and she looked away. I felt fabric brush my arm as she smoothed the sleeve of what was probably a super ugly hospital gown.

"Sweetie, it's a miracle you're still here with us. They said we might lose you." Her voice broke. "We didn't give up though—and look at you now!"

"I look that good, huh?" It was the best I could do at humor, to try to cheer her. I bet I looked horrible, because I was beginning to realize I felt that way. My entire body ached, and my right jawline burned.

"You look like an angel to me." She brushed some hair off my face. "But you'll feel better when you're not in that hospital bed. Now you're awake, we can work toward getting you out of here and home where you belong." She smiled the way she did when she was being sad and brave at the same time.

I grinned weakly up at her, I think, but felt completely exhausted. I probably fell asleep again.

After that, there were many times I'd wake up and realize I was in the hospital and Mom or Dad was sitting by my bed. One time Grandma Reba was there instead.

"Hey, Gran."

"Hey, yourself." Her blue eyes sparkled with a mischievous challenge. "Are you going to stay in that bed forever, Emily Elizabeth?"

I chuckled, which by this time only hurt a little bit. "I hope not."

"That's good to hear. What *are* you going to do?"

The answer to her question depended on Adam who hadn't been here any of the times I was conscious. Surely, he was making plans to take me home to our apartment. He'd better not let me down.

"Go home, I guess." Meaning the place I shared with my boyfriend, but I didn't say it that way because I knew Gran didn't approve.

She frowned, something Gran seldom does.

"You've been given a second chance, Emily. Best be using it wisely."

A tall, dark-skinned man came in, wearing a white lab coat. As he walked, his focus moved back and forth between the clipboard he held and the phone he was texting on. He stopped at my bed and seemed surprised to see us.

"Well. This is lovely. The grandmother is visiting?"

Gran nodded. "Are you her doctor?"

"Yes, yes. One of them. Miss Emily Kincaid, you have come back from the dead. Very nice." He glanced at the clipboard and back up, meeting my eyes. "Concussion, internal injuries, and a severe right tibial fracture." He must have noticed my lack of understanding. "Shin bone. Your lower right leg is fractured." He gently turned my face to one side with his long fingers. "And this scar to help you remember." His grin was unnaturally white, but his deep brown eyes were friendly. "So you must now begin to work. This will be hard work, Miss Emily. You will tire easily and become frustrated." He wrote something across the paper on the clipboard. "But it cannot be helped. We start at this very low point." He nodded and looked at my grandmother. "Your name, dear lady?"

Gran brightened, looking immediately younger at

the handsome doctor's attention. "I'm Reba Markland." She held out her hand, and he took it solemnly. For a grandma, she did look pretty awesome with her silver hair in a pixie cut, and a complexion that had never spent time lying out in the sun.

"Ah. Miss Reba Markland, it is a decided pleasure to make your acquaintance. I am called Dr. Jay. I have noticed your presence here many times since this fine girl came to us."

"Of course. I've been here many times." Gran retrieved her hand slowly, her face glowing with pleasure. "Emily is part mine." She looked at me and winked.

After beaming at her for a long moment, Dr. Jay turned back to me. "Miss Emily Kincaid, you have a very nice family. Also, two teenage sisters." His delight faded briefly, and I wondered what the twins had said or done to make an impression. With them, the possibilities were endless.

"This is important," he said, writing again. "Your very nice family will be a help to you in recovering."

"Just what will that involve?" I didn't want to commit without knowing first what Dr. Jay had in mind.

"You will be up to sit in a chair a bit today with

therapy at your side. This will be done, and when you are stable, you will transfer to rehab. When you can safely function, you go home." He took a moment to read something on his phone, and when he looked up again, his big brown eyes pinned me. "Miss Emily, one does not visit death and return to the living without change. You are beginning a new life. Proceed with gratitude."

Clueless of an appropriate response, I nodded at him, and he did the same to me. He took Gran's hand again, bowed slightly, and left.

"That was weird." I pitched my voice low to be sure he couldn't hear me if he was still outside the door.

Gran shook her head. "Not really. He just has a bit of difficulty with the language. I only know one language and so do you. I'm always impressed with those who know more."

"Uh, no. I meant it was weird what he said about beginning a new life."

She took a deep breath. "You do realize the wreck nearly—killed you?"

Why did everybody have to mention my close scrape with death as if it was news to me? I wanted to scream—*put the past where it belongs and get me out of here!*

I cleared my throat, forcing my voice to remain calm. "I get that I was in bad shape."

"You were given a fifty-fifty chance, Emily. Do not take this lightly. The fact that we are having any type of conversation at this moment is miraculous. Take Dr. Jay's advice. Proceed with gratitude." She closed the magazine that lay ignored on her lap. "Then decide how you're going to *live* your life. Enough of simply existing."

I sighed and turned my head toward the window, remembering the dream about sitting on the hill in a field of daisies. The scene was still beautifully vivid in my mind, but I hadn't mentioned the experience to anyone, afraid of spoiling its perfection. Though I liked to think of the dream as a glimpse of heaven, it was just as likely induced by pain meds. Either way, I would keep my secret, hugging the memory tightly when I felt despondent, which was often.

And no amount of being preached at about gratitude was going to make me feel better. I was in pain, bored with the hospital, and missing my boyfriend.

Turn the page, Emily.

Although I'd heard it before when Gran wasn't there and knew it wasn't her voice, there was no one else in the room, so I turned back and looked at Gran.

She was gathering a large knitting project and her magazines, sliding them into her massive tote bag.

"Did you hear that?" I whispered.

She glanced at me as she slid her arms into her coat sleeves. "Hear what?"

"Oh…nothing." I wanted an explanation for the voice, yet was afraid to explore for it. "Um. You're leaving already, Gran?"

"I've been here six hours, Emily. You slept most of the time, but I'm ready to go home and flop into a *comfortable* chair." She picked up the black velvet tote with bright shapes stitched onto it in an eccentric pattern. "Your parents will be here in a little while, honey. I'll let you tell them your news." Leaning down, she kissed my cheek. "I'll see you very soon. I love you, Emily Elizabeth."

"Love you too, Gran."

My parents arrived, looking tired and rushed. I wondered how many times they had driven the forty minutes to visit me here, even when I was unconscious and didn't know they were around. At any rate, I could see the whole experience had taken a toll on both of them, as it had on Gran. But it wasn't like I'd asked them to make the trip so often, right?

"Hey, guys. Good news from Dr. Jay. Have you

met him?"

They nodded.

Dad slipped off his coat and helped Mom with hers. "He and the other doctors in his office have been impressive. What's the news?"

"I get out of bed today, and before long, I should be out of here."

They looked doubtful. "I'll go to the nurses' station," Mom said and left.

Dad tossed the coats onto the chair Gran had vacated. He perched cautiously on the edge of my bed and took my hand in his big one.

I was hurt by their reaction—or rather, lack of it. "Mom doesn't believe me?"

He shrugged. "We've learned to check at the nurses' station after talking to a doctor. Sometimes we've been so overwhelmed by everything, it's been difficult to take in the information the doctors give. Checking to see what's written on the chart is a reassurance or helps us clarify."

I sagged into the pillow. "I'm sorry for what I've put you through, Dad."

"No need to apologize. Your focus should be on

getting stronger, Emily."

"You've got it. I want to get out of here and get on with life." Such as it was.

"Has Adam been in to see you?" Dad's voice was casual as he re-arranged the ugly privacy curtain.

"Not that I'm aware of. I mean, if he was here, it was when I was asleep." I sighed. "Probably not."

"That's no way for a young man in love to behave."

"Maybe he's sick and doesn't want to give me a germ." Whatever. I didn't want to think deeply about my boyfriend's absence or have this conversation—the one that started with—*Why do you always choose that kind of guy? The irresponsible kind. The ones who aren't worthy of you?*

I'd heard those words many times through the years. From my parents, siblings, friends. And with Gran it was even worse—she could just look at me a certain way and I knew what she was thinking. No doubt she compared all my boyfriends to my grandpa, who'd been like this ideal husband, father, grandfather, important citizen in the community, and all that. I had loved Grandpa Geoffrey, but his memory would be hard for anyone to live up to, especially the losers I seemed to gravitate to.

Mom's face was flushed with excitement when she came in after getting the details from the nurses. "Marcus, the nurse says once Emily is able to get up into a wheelchair and her temperature stays normal, she can be moved to Meadowbrooke for rehabilitation. It's just a few miles from here. Easy to get to from the flyer they gave me." She was clutching the flyer in one hand and gently put it in mine. How pathetic is it to see your mom excited about moving you to a nursing home?

Without looking at the paper, I pushed it away and it fluttered to the floor. Again, I had to force my voice to sound normal, even when I felt I was about to lose it. "You must be kidding. I'm not going there."

"Yes, you are." Dad's 'no-nonsense' look had appeared. "In anticipation of the doctor's statement today, I've already talked with several of the staff here and done a little research. Meadowbrooke's rehab department has a great reputation." He scooped up the flyer and deposited it on the table by my bed. "We need to be thankful for this step in the right direction, instead of ruining it from the outset with the wrong attitude."

I took a deep breath, curled my nails into my palms when what I wanted to do was pound on something in frustration. "I'm *twenty-five*, not eighty-five. I'm *not* going to a nursing home."

His face was suddenly as forbidding as winter storm clouds. "I know a lot of people over eighty who are in better shape right now than you are, Emily. You will go to Meadowbrooke and work hard, and when you're well enough, you can come home."

Frowning right back at him, I barely managed to keep my thoughts to myself for the moment. It felt as if they were pushing me away, not wanting to deal with me when I wasn't able to do everything for myself. Well, the good news for them was that I wasn't going to their house after I was better. I was going to Adam's, once he got off his butt and took some initiative. They had conveniently managed to forget that fact, and I would just let it ride for now.

Mom was still smiling. "They're sending physical therapy in a few minutes to get you up, Emily." She took a bathrobe out of the meager closet space, draped it over my knees, and pushed the bed control to slowly raise me into a sitting position.

A stoic looking woman soon appeared, carrying an aluminum walker. "Hello. I'm June. I understand Dr. Jay has told you about starting P.T. today."

We muttered agreement.

"Good." She nodded, made use of the hand sanitizer, and looked at her watch. "An aide will be here soon to assist me." June was my mom's age or more and had deeply etched frown lines between brows that could have used some shaping. She cleared her throat and looked at the clock on the wall, focused on doing her job and not on chatter. That worked for me—I wanted to check this physical therapy thing off my list so I could get out of here.

"Hey, June." A stocky girl with swinging dark hair bounced into the room. Her face was a giant smile, and I immediately disliked her for it. "Hey, everybody. I'm Kim. They told me Emily's ready to start P.T. How great is that?"

Staring at her, I tried to recall meeting her before. "Do I know you?"

"I'm Kim," she said more slowly this time. "Don't know if you remember me, but I've been in to help with you a bunch of times. You were asleep a lot."

Wow. There's news.

"I remember you, Kim," Mom said cheerfully enough for all of us. "Thanks to both of you for coming in so quickly. We think it's wonderful news the doctor wants Emily to start getting out of bed."

"I bet. Since she was almost dead and all." Kim winked at me. "But not quite dead, right, Emily?" While I glared at them, they efficiently got me swiveled around and gently lowered my legs off the bed. "And not as far gone as Westley in *The Princess Bride*." My legs were dangling over the side of the bed now, and

Mom rushed to put slippers on my feet. I think she was trying to be gentle, but it hurt so much I bit my lip to keep from shrieking. Suddenly I was dizzy and my stomach began to roll with queasiness. I was in pitiful shape if sitting up in bed had this effect.

June spoke briefly to Kim, her voice so low I couldn't hear.

Kim nodded understanding and resumed chatting to me and my parents. "So we don't have as much of a project as Miracle Max had. Now…if you were *mostly dead*, this would *really* be a challenge." Deep dimples appeared in Kim's cheeks and her dark eyes sparkled as she chuckled at the movie reference. I knew that old movie too and steeled myself not to be taken in by Kim's cheerfulness.

To move things along and get Kim out of my face, I started to push off the bed, but they stopped me.

"Take a moment," June directed. "Breathe slowly and deeply."

Kim's smile widened. "No magic pill here. Your rehab is going to require lots of hard work."

I stared into her eyes. "Are you playing the part of Andre the Giant in this epic?"

Mom gasped, and Kim took a deep breath. "Whatever works to get your motor running, Emily.

You need to say ugly things to me, go ahead. I'm just doing my job. Or you could be pleasant. Up to you."

I didn't want to be pleasant. I wanted to be left alone—or even better, to just be okay again. Nobody seemed to know who or what had caused the wreck, so I was angry without anything in particular to direct the anger toward. The giant, day-at-a-time calendar on the wall told me I'd lost two weeks of my life flat on my back in this stupid hospital. It was mid-November already.

June re-positioned my hands on the walker. "Do *not* put any weight on your right leg, Emily. Ready? Here we go!"

I tried not to but couldn't help yelling. The pain was incredible.

"Emily!" Mom was instantly at my side. "June, should she be up if it hurts this much?"

"Doctor's orders," June said softly, while helping support me.

Kim added, "From what the doctors and nurses say, she's gonna hurt for a long time. Lucky to be alive." She looked from Mom to me. "You don't feel lucky right now, I bet."

No way would I try to answer. Tears streamed down my face as I stood there, clutching the walker.

Chapter Three

Intense pain seemed to be everywhere but especially in my right leg.

June muttered softly, "Lean on the walker. Keep your right foot off the ground. Scoot your left foot."

I did and nearly passed out from the pain. But Dr. Jay had given orders, and I would get up in that chair even if it killed me. What a shame he wasn't here now, because I had a few choice words I'd like to share with him. All in all, the experience of hopping from my bed to the chair was horrendous.

I sat in the chair, wishing I were in bed and that I could get there without having to reverse the process that had placed me in this spot. My parents tried to engage me in conversation, but I have no idea what was discussed. I was just thinking about how much I hurt.

A very long hour later, the June and Kim team returned.

"I think that's enough for now," June said. "We'll try again later, Emily."

It seemed to take forever, but arriving back at my hospital bed was a huge relief. They helped me sit down and lifted my legs. They left, having folded the walker and stowed it in a corner, and I started to breathe easier now that I was once again flat on my back. I realized I was covered in a cold sweat.

Mom slid the tray table back into position and poured fresh ice water from the plastic pitcher into my cup. With a shaky hand, I picked it up and managed to aim the straw at my mouth. After a couple of sips, I sighed. "Okay, I guess I need rehab. That was easily the worst experience of my life."

"Watching it ranks right up there for me too," Dad said, looking anguished. Mom had her back to me now, and I assumed from the way her shoulders shook that she was crying.

***

That's the day it began—being dragged out of bed twice a day, hopping back and forth to the stupid chair and sitting there a little longer each time. It always required the assistance of a physical therapist and an aide with quick reflexes, because my right leg sometimes did weird stuff without warning. To their credit, I never hit the floor, though I suspect they might have liked to see me fall.

One morning Kim bounced into the room, her bright smile firmly in place. "You're outta here, Emily!"

"I'm—what?"

"Dr. Jay said you're going to be released today to go to Meadowbrooke. I bet you're excited." She bustled around getting me ready for yet another Walk of Pain. She stopped and peered into my eyes. "I don't get it. Aren't you happy?"

I met her gaze. "Seriously? Would you be happy about going to a nursing home?"

She crossed her arms and took a half step back. "Off the record, and only because you asked, let me tell you this. You puzzle me, Emily. You're alive in spite of internal and orthopedic injuries that were bad enough to kill you. Usually when someone comes back from being that near death, it's because they have a strong desire to live. It's because they *fought* for a second chance." She shook her head. "You don't seem to care. You don't seem grateful or glad to be alive."

"What do you know about it? Everything is

different for me since that wreck. Don't I get a chance to adjust to being a cripple?"

Always Cheerful Kim looked at me with distaste. "I know something about having your normal world suddenly snatched away. Here's a news flash for you, Emily: Bad stuff happens. Learn to deal." She took a breath and seemed to make a decision. "My guess is your life has been pretty easy up until now." She paused, maybe expecting me to reply, but I didn't. "It's my job to do my best to help you, but here's a piece of free advice. Cherish every moment you've got. Even the pain is a reminder that you're alive." Her eyes filled with tears. "There are so many people who would have loved a chance like you're getting." She turned and walked quickly from the room, nearly colliding with June in the doorway.

Shaking her head, June watched her go. When she stepped fully into the room, she was glaring at me. It didn't require a lot of imagination to read her thoughts: *Everyone's favorite patient is being released today. Hallelujah.*

Kim didn't return and after a while another aide arrived to help June get me into the dreaded chair. Something had struck a chord with Kim, but that wasn't my fault. She needed to toughen up if she wanted to work in a hospital. And she had no business lecturing me in the first place.

***

Dr. Jay came in when I was sitting in the chair. "Well, Miss Emily. Are you ready for your next step to recovery?"

"I doubt it. But since I don't get to make the decisions, I'm headed to the nursing home." Fabulous rehab facility or not, I was still angry about having to go to the dreaded Meadowbrooke. Since Adam hadn't done anything about coming to get me and take me back to our place—or, indeed, about coming to see me at all—my only option was to endure Meadowbrooke and then, theoretically, go to my parents' home. How could I return there to live at my age? That plan was beyond messed up, and I needed to figure out a different option by the time I was released from rehab.

Dr. Jay forced a grin. "This is discharge day, Miss Emily. If your attitude is good, your progress will be easier. With hard work in rehab, your return home will occur sooner." He paused a moment, studying my face. "This is not pleasing to you?"

"Be more pleasing without the rehab," I muttered.

"Ah, but you badly need it. The people at Meadowbrooke are very wonderful. Attitude makes all the difference. This you must know." He patted my hand. "The next time we meet, I hope you will be making wonderful progress in rehabilitation." He tipped his head in farewell, turned on his heel, and hit the hand sanitizer on the way out.

A couple of seconds later, the door opened again, and I got ready to bark at whoever it was. I bit my tongue when my two best friends walked in.

"Hey, girl. Lookin' better today." My friend Danielle said it, and Karly nodded agreement as they sauntered into the room wearing the latest fashion and cute, spike-heeled boots. The three of us have been BFFs our entire lives, but I hated them for their freedom right now.

I reached up and ran my fingers through my hair. "I haven't seen a mirror lately, but I'm guessing that's a lie."

They took off their jackets and piled them on the window sill. Karly hopped onto the side of my bed, while Danielle collapsed into a nearby chair.

"She didn't say you look *good*, Emily. Just better." Karly took a pack of gum out of her bag and offered it around. It tasted amazing after days of hospital food. "Seriously, that scar along your jaw is scary. What do they say about it?"

I shrugged. "I may never make the Miss America contest. I'm coping with the disappointment. Even more exciting is where I'm headed today." I wadded up the wrapper, tossed it, and missed the trash can by a mile. The effort to throw made me groan.

"Right. Nursing home—sweet." Danielle popped her gum. "You'll have all those little old men chasing you in their wheelchairs. The little old ladies will be jealous and hate you. It should be a hoot."

Karly winked. "Think of it like this, Emily. You're doing them all a favor by shaking things up while you're there."

"I'd rather do them all a favor some other way. Some way that doesn't involve me actually going there." I hated the idea more each second.

My dad came into the room, handsome and smooth as ever. The girls beamed at him stupidly as if he were George Clooney.

"Emily, you're not going to be there long-term. Just for a little while," he said.

"Can't I just go home, Dad? Please? I can do exercises and stuff there. I promise I'll work hard." Even going to my parents' house, which I wanted to avoid, would be better than a nursing home.

"Emily, we want you home, but this is the best way. I've talked it over with some people I know who've been in Meadowbrooke, and they agree residential rehab will get you back to normal function sooner." He lightly squeezed both of my hands. "I have an idea you're going to be highly motivated while you're there and exceed expectations. You've surprised the doctors here."

Dead silence as we all thought about that statement. I hadn't won any friends with my griping. I also wasn't sure what "normal function" would be for me. It wasn't as if I'd had much of a life going before the wreck, so normal function shouldn't require a lot of time in the lockup. That's what I had decided to call Meadowbrooke Rehabilitation Facility—the lockup. So much for Dr. Jay's suggestion of working on my attitude.

"Be back in a minute, Emily." Dad headed back out into the hall on some kind of a mission.

"Where will you go afterward?" Karly asked. "After Meadowbrooke, I mean. I notice you said 'home.'" She and Danielle watched me expectantly.

"What do you think?"

"Adam's?" Karly suggested and her eyebrows rose with the question mark. Danielle said nothing but slowly shook her head.

"Girls, this sucks, but I don't know. Adam hasn't exactly been a regular visitor."

"Maybe hospitals make him nervous," said Karly

with encouragement. "And he'll be more comfortable visiting you at the rehab."

"Maybe he's been working a lot," Danielle offered. We both looked at her in disbelief, and she giggled. "Okay. That's gotta be wrong. Maybe he's worked so little that he can't afford the gas to drive here."

Karly nodded. "That sounds more like Adam." She shrugged, frowning. "But if he wanted to come down, he'd find a ride."

"I'm giving him some time to get his head around my situation. Maybe when he was here and saw me unconscious and hooked to a bunch of tubes and stuff, he got scared."

"Well, yeah. It was scary for all of us," said Danielle. "But it's not like we would just give up on you." A tone sounded. She looked at her phone and sent a quick update to someone. "When are your parents going to get you another phone? Being without one is prehistoric."

"I know. It's weird not to be able to just text you. I guess my phone was lost in the corn field where the car landed. I asked Dad about it. Not sure if the phone company is giving them grief about a free replacement or what. I'll ask again soon." Much as I wanted one, I knew Mom and Dad had plenty on their plate and weren't worried about my social media needs.

Danielle looked down when another tone sounded and dealt with it. "Having a phone would make the nursing home so much easier to take."

I glared at her. "It's not a nursing home. It's a rehabilitation facility."

"Right. We'll be there to visit you as often as we can," Karly said, and Danielle nodded. "Maybe we can help nudge your parents about the phone too."

Danielle said, "If Adam doesn't come through for you, what's Plan B?"

"I don't have a Plan B yet."

"What? You always need a backup, girlfriend."

"Yeah, well, I don't have one. Not this time. I don't even want to say my parents' house is an option. Going back there to live would be such a step backward."

"True. But a lot of people our age are doing it when they hit hard times."

"I need to move on with my life." It wasn't just me saying that. It was the doctor and Gran, Mom and Dad, and the offensive Always Cheerful Kim.

"I hear you, Emily. But move on to where? And what? No place to live. No job."

"Thanks loads. That seems to cover my situation pretty well. But something has to come along."

"You could move in with us, but you can't. I mean, we'd love it, but the landlord would throw us all out. We can't afford to break the lease either."

"Not a problem." Their place was miniscule. There was barely enough room for the two of them.

I leaned an elbow on the walker which was parked next to my chair. "I'd love to be on my own somewhere. Wouldn't that be cool?" I had never had my own place, somewhere for just me. Now that I said it out loud, I realized how desperately I wanted it.

Dad returned with backup this time. June was beside him, looking as if she'd rather be anywhere else, along with a new-to-me nurse aide with a linebacker physique.

"Time to go, Emily," June said. "Girls, you'll excuse us?"

Danielle and Karly shrugged into their jackets and left, turning back toward me and holding thumbs up as they exited the room. I gave them the signal back, feeling anything but encouraged.

Chapter Four

"What do you remember about the accident, Emily?" Steven, a counselor in the lockup asked.

"I told you before—nothing. I woke up in the hospital."

"Are you sure? Relax for a minute and try to think back."

As if I didn't think about it pretty much twenty-four/seven. "You think I haven't tried to remember the accident that put me in the hospital and landed me here? I can't. I've tried like a million times."

"There wasn't fog that night."

Oh goody. The weather report again. I drummed my fingers on the arms of my chair. "Oka-aaay."

"It wasn't raining. It was cold, but the road

surfaces were dry so no ice to cause you to lose control."

I felt like standing up and screaming at him, except my demonstration of pique wouldn't be very impressive since, without some assistance, the standing-up part would take me a while, if I could successfully manage it at all. So I tried to stare a hole through him.

He smiled encouragingly. "I'm just trying to help."

"That's nice, Steven." I honored him with a smirk. "I don't remember the accident. You sitting there, peering at me like I *should* remember makes me feel insanely angry. Is that a breakthrough of any sort? And, if so, can we adjourn for today?"

His pleasant demeanor remained, completely unaffected by my outburst. I wanted to wipe that smug grin off his face.

"Where are you going from here, Emily?"

My good leg started to tap the floor impatiently. "I don't know, Steven. I'm keeping my options open."

"Adam?"

"How—? Do you know Adam?"

"Not know him. I've heard his name. He hasn't been here to see you since you came to

Meadowbrooke." Steven wrote something on a little pad of paper or maybe he was just drawing doodles. "How would you describe your relationship with Adam?"

I willed my heartbeat to return to its normal cadence. "I wouldn't describe it at all. Not to you anyway."

"Why not?"

"Because I don't want to." I took a breath. "Short version, Adam and I are in love."

Steven frowned sympathetically.

"I don't need your pity. Adam will come here for me and take me home. He doesn't care about rules or what a bossy doctor says. He'll come here and check me out and take me home."

He never did, the rat. Not only didn't he come to pick me up, he never even visited. When my parents brought me a new phone, I called him. He let it go to voice mail but didn't call back. No matter how many voicemails I left, the mailbox never got full, meaning he was deleting and ignoring my messages. I sent a few texts, but soon gave up on the one-way conversation. I still had *some* pride, after all.

***

"Em'ly!" Matthew Singer ran in through the front entryway of the lockup, having spotted me on one of my walks in the hall.

"Matthew." His mom, Melissa, spoke his name calmly and without shouting, in that warning tone that effective moms have. He stopped, looked back at her, and changed his pace to a sedate walk toward me.

"Hey, Matthew. Did you come all the way down here to visit me?"

"Yes! I comed to cheer you *up!* Okay?"

"Yeah, okay. That's sure what I need." The therapist who had been walking with me made certain I was safely in a chair before she excused herself. I reached out both arms to Matthew. After giving me a gentle hug, he stood leaning against my chair with one hand on my arm.

He handed me a slightly crumpled paper and looked up into my eyes. "I miss you, Em'ly. Mommy said they take care of you, but I still miss you."

I leaned down and kissed his cheek. "You're the sweetest guy, Matthew Singer. You know that? And I've sure missed you."

His face lit up. "Mommy! Did you hear it?"

Melissa grinned and nodded. "I did."

I looked at the paper Matthew had given me. It was just regular sheet of copy paper folded in half, and on the outside my name was printed above a drawing of a simple daisy—green stem and a leaf, big black swoops for petals around the fat yellow center. Inside, he had carefully printed his first name. "Wow, Matthew. Did you make this?"

"Yes, I drawed it for you. To make you feel better." He patted my hand. "Do you feel better?"

"I sure do." I hugged him tightly and got a good long whiff of his little boy aroma. "Thanks so much. I'm gonna keep this card forever."

His face glowed.

Melissa sat in a chair across from me. "How are you, Emily? Is there a lot of pain?"

"Yes, but not as much as there was at first. I'm making progress, they say."

She tipped her head. "You surprised the doctors."

"Yes."

"You've been given a second chance at life. That's special."

It was frustrating to have this topic brought up again. I didn't know what to do with my second chance.

So far it was full of feeling terrible—physically from the injuries and mentally from Adam ignoring me.

Lost in my thoughts, I hadn't been listening to Melissa.

"...So you're welcome to stay with us. You know we have loads of room." I looked from her to Matthew who was barely managing to contain his excitement. I had been the little guy's babysitter for a few weeks before my accident and loved him. Yet I couldn't imagine how the three of us would coexist at this point. The physical therapists had told me I wouldn't be one hundred percent for a few months. The counselor Steven and I weren't exactly bonding, and I doubted he thought I would ever attain mental normalcy, whatever that might mean.

"Oh, gee, Melissa, that's so kind of you. I mean, wow, that's awesome. I...um...it will be a while before I'm good at doing steps on my own. Could be a little awkward."

"We don't care, Em'ly. We want you to stay with us." Matthew clapped a hand over his mouth and his eyes shot to his mom. Obviously, he'd been instructed not to push.

I hugged him again. "Let me think about it. I have to ace a test to get out of here."

Melissa nodded, looking around at the clean, bright lobby. "Meadowbrooke didn't exist when I left the area. It's a nice facility. I'm sure it wouldn't be feasible to have a rehab in little Serendipity, but the drive isn't bad."

"My family has made it a lot of times. At least one of them is here every day. Same with the hospital as far as I know." I shook my head. "I slept a lot. I feel bad about all the trouble I've been."

She leaned on the arm rest, her eyes on Matthew. "I'm sure you would do the same for any of them if they were here."

I thought about her statement. Would I have been so diligent in caring for a family member as they had done for me? Or would I have behaved more like my absent boyfriend?

I cleared my throat. "Adam hasn't been to visit me since I transferred from the hospital."

She nodded slowly. "Yes, your mom said something like that. Not that it's any of my business."

"Hey, we're from Serendipity, where everything is everybody's business."

Melissa nodded. "I'm not used to that yet. I lived away long enough to forget some of the intricacies of small town life." She took a breath. "Is there anything you need? Matthew and I can go to one of the big box stores around here and pick it up."

I shrugged. "I don't know what it would be. I have loose-fitting clothes and non-skid house shoes." I pulled up a pants leg so my shoe was more visible. "I can't even call them house slippers, because they won't— slip." I chuckled lamely.

Matthew didn't get the joke, and Melissa looked sad.

I sat up straighter, squared my shoulders. "Thanks for asking, Melissa. There's nothing I need that can be bought in a store."

She nodded. "There's wisdom in that statement."

Not as much as she thought. It isn't that I was trying to be deeply philosophical. I wanted Adam to come and get me. I wanted Adam to want me.

But, evidently, that was too much to ask. And that hurt.

***

Danielle and Karly took their sweet time arriving for their first visit at the lockup. When they finally did, I'd nearly given up on them.

"Hey." They sidled into my room, looking

uncomfortable.

"Hey. I thought maybe you guys had been abducted by aliens or something."

They shrugged. "Been busy with stuff," Karly rocked from one bright-red, stiletto ankle boot to the other. Did they *have* to wear the cutest, most enviable footwear every time they visited me?

"Oh. Well that certainly explains it."

"Adam says hey." Danielle blurted out, and Karly elbowed her in the side.

"He does, huh? Does he say anything else? Is he going to get his sorry butt down here to visit?"

"Don't think so, Emily. He's got a new job. He works nights, so he sleeps a lot during the daytime."

I waited for the rest of the story. They looked uncomfortable about something. "What is it? What's really up?"

"Adam decided he needs to make a fresh start, Emily. The two of you... Well, we all knew that wouldn't work, right?"

"I didn't." I looked at both of my good friends. Was there more they weren't telling me?

"Come on, Emily. All your relationships fall apart

eventually."

"The ones in the past, sure. Everybody has a past. But Adam and I had something special."

Karly twisted a handful of her long, white-blond hair. "He packed up your stuff. He told us a couple of days after the wreck, he packed it up. It's in your parents' garage."

"Awesome. I have a wreck and almost die, and Adam decides this is the time to break up with me?"

"I think it's been coming on for a while," Danielle said. Karly nodded vigorously.

"But he didn't want anybody to tell you right away. In case it would kill you or something."

I wiped tears off my cheeks. "That's considerate of him. What a guy. Did Adam know the two of you were coming here to give me the news?"

Danielle's face flushed. "Yeah. We saw him the other day, and he said he needed to text you about it. Can you believe that? *Text you.* We said we would tell you in person. He's such a loser. You're lucky to know it now instead of later." Her eyes strayed desperately around the room. "Hey! Wheelchair." She grabbed the handles and started toward me. "Want us to push you around?"

"I'm tired of being pushed around. Ha ha."

Karly brightened. "Oh, come on, Emily. You can see from the window that it's a pretty day outside. We'll push you out into the garden."

"It's what, twenty degrees out? And this time of November, everything is brown and gray. No thanks."

"Oh, the temp is probably close to sixty. Pretty decent for this time of year. Do you have a coat? Or we can bundle you up in blankets."

"No thanks, girls. I'll stay in here. I am just fine. I have my hospital bed, hideous slippers, a wardrobe of easy-on-and-off clothing for old people, and my regulation cable TV setup with a million channels of nothing."

Danielle was near tears. "We just want to help. To cheer you up."

"I know it, Danielle, but I'm not in the mood right now to be a cheerful patient."

"Are you ever?" asked Karly, looking frustrated.

"Actually, no."

At that precise moment, the last person in the world I wanted to see bounced into the room. Just when I thought I was free of Always Cheerful Kim's bright outlook on life, she followed me to Meadowbrooke.

"Hey there, Emily. Have they done that personality transplant on you yet?"

"*Kim*?"

She touched her heart dramatically. "You remembered me. How flattering. Or is it just my resemblance to Andre the Giant that tipped you off?"

I groaned, silently I hoped, remembering what I had said to her the first day she entered my life, so chipper I wanted to choke her.

She dropped her hand, enjoying my discomfiture. "No matter. I'm here, and as The Force would have it, I've been assigned to your section of the facility. What joy that will be for both of us." She glanced at Karly and Danielle, who stood open-mouthed, watching us spar. "You girls here to visit?"

They nodded.

"Okay, then visit. If she's in a worse mood when you leave than she is now, I'll be on your case next time I see you. Got that?"

They nodded again, vigorously.

Karly pointed to the wheelchair in the corner. "We were trying to cheer her up. Take her for a ride in that."

Kim frowned and shook her head. "She doesn't need to be riding around like a movie star at detox. She needs to be working her sorry muscles." She seared me with a look. "Are you trying *at all* to make progress, Emily?"

"Of course, I'm trying. I want to get out of here. I want it more than ever, now that you're here. And *why are you here?*"

She smiled again, showing every single tooth. "I'm part-time at the hospital now. They cut my hours. So I got a part-time job here too. Sweet, huh? Same number of hours, less pay, and no benefits. But you know what? Life's good, Emily Kincaid. You try to remember that."

While she talked, she cleaned away remnants of my recent snack, dealt with a wash cloth I'd left on the bathroom door handle, took my robe off the foot of the bed and hung it in the closet, and straightened everything in the room. She sailed out into the hallway, humming "Ding-Dong the Witch is Dead" from *The Wizard of Oz*.

"Oh. My. Gosh." Karly looked at me, then at Danielle. They started to giggle and were soon laughing.

"What in the world is so funny? You think having Always Cheerful Kim here is amusing? She's horrible."

47

"She's awesome, Emily. She's bright and funny and—yeah—cheerful. And she is going to kick your butt." Danielle grinned. "And you thought you wanted out of here before." They started to laugh again.

I didn't pay much attention to them. I just sat there fuming at the coincidence that had brought Kim to Meadowbrooke and wondered about her strange cheerfulness at losing her full-time status and bennies at the hospital. She was one of the weirdest people I'd ever met.

***

"Okay, Princess." The overhead light was suddenly blazing into my face. I squeezed my eyelids tight and rolled over on my side. I couldn't stifle the groan of pain that came with that movement. "Today you're going to do three rounds of every hall in this building plus a workout in the gym with Leo, the head of PT. Won't that be fun?" Kim raised the head of my bed, which forced me to roll fully onto my back again. I glared at her, and she winked. "Need to potty before you head down to breakfast? Better be quick about it. We're on a tight schedule." She bounced toward the doorway, not waiting for my response to anything. "Need help, call. Otherwise, I have other mornings to brighten."

Muttering under my breath, I slid my feet into my house shoes and tottered to the bathroom with my

48

walker. When I had washed my hands and returned to my room, I was already tired and ready to lie down again.

She popped back into the doorway. "There you are. Good job getting this far on your own, Emily. Shall I find some clothes for you?"

"No thanks. If you could just shut the door and keep it shut, I'm capable of getting dressed." Kim started to hum as she'd done before, pulled the curtain halfheartedly to its end-stop which in theory is supposed to grant some amount of privacy. Lucky for me, I'd lost what little modesty I'd had before the wreck. With all the doctors, nurses, aides, etc., who had seen every inch of me, I didn't much care who saw what from here on out.

Just as I got my shirt buttoned and had started the miserable process of pulling on my pants, someone tapped lightly on the door. "What?" I yelled.

Seeing David Standish's handsome face peeking around the edge of the door was one of the biggest surprises ever. I'd had a major teenage crush on him back in the day.

"Emily? You decent in there?"

"Uh, no. Wait a minute." I finished pulling on the black stretchy pants, huffing and puffing with the effort.

Unfortunately, I knew I looked like crap. "Okay. You can come in, David."

He stepped into the room hesitantly, incongruous in the Modern Medicine Style room in his GQ business casual. For an older guy, he sure looked good. Maybe I'd been away from Adam too long—or from any man who wasn't wearing scrubs and making me work hard.

I ran a hand through my hair. "This is a nice surprise. What brings you to my nightmare?"

He chuckled, pulling a vase of white daisies from behind his back. "I saw these and decided they needed a home with someone who would appreciate them."

"Oh. So pretty. I *love* daisies." I took the vase and gently touched one of the delicate petals.

"Yes, I know. I have my sources." He looked around the room. "Okay if I sit down for a minute? Not long—I'm on the way to the airport, of course."

"Ah. Of course. What else, huh?"

"Yep. So, how are you? You look—well, Emily, you look really beat."

"I feel it. Thanks for the honesty, although I wouldn't have minded a little white lie."

"Sorry." He grinned. "How long do you think

you'll be here? Is the rehab going well?"

"I'm doing better than I was, but not sure when I can leave. Believe it or not, simply being able to dress myself is a pretty big deal, even if it does take half the morning to accomplish."

"I do believe it's a big deal, considering how badly you were hurt." He shook his head solemnly. "I hope you don't mind me dropping in like this. The nurse said you had to get down to breakfast and had a full schedule. She said I shouldn't take too long."

"She did, did she?" That Kim was on my last nerve. "This nurse—did you notice her name? Was she really, really happy?"

"Sorry. I didn't notice." He stood. "How about I walk you down to breakfast? Is that allowed?"

"Oh. Well—sure, I guess. I just need to get ol' Silver." I slowly stood and took hold of the walker with both hands and started toward the door.

David winced when he saw me with the walker, but I didn't want pity. "This isn't as bad as it looks, David. I'll be riding my bike before you know it." Saying those words sounded more hopeful than I'd been feeling so far.

He let me go through the doorway first and matched my slow pace.

"I'm glad to hear that. I'll look forward to seeing you ride up my driveway."

Yeah, me too. There was a weird fluttering sensation in my stomach, and this conversation felt more like flirting than I'd ever have expected with David Standish.

"So, David. Um. What's new with you? Still traveling all week, every week?"

"Yep. Except for Thanksgiving through Christmas. As in, when I get home this week, I'm around for a month. What a perfect life, huh?"

David was in marketing, which required him to be gone a lot. But one month of the year he was a fulltime employee of the Standish Christmas Tree Farm, the family business and also the place he called home.

"Wow. It is almost Thanksgiving, isn't it?" I gestured at a fall decoration we walked by. "Guess I should pay a little more attention to the passage of time. You're serious, right? You do still like what you're doing? You've had that same job all my life."

He sighed. "Not quite all your life. You make me sound ancient."

"Oops. Sorry." Ancient but suddenly yummy looking. He also smelled delicious.

"Okay. No more references to our slight age difference, please. Ten years is no big deal. And about work—yes, it's all good. Sometimes I get tired of the travel, but I love the job." He shot me a sideways glance which I caught because I'd been watching him. "One snag. My house is kind of a wreck."

I laughed. "I'll bet it is. Can't find anybody crazy enough to go in there every Thursday with a scoop shovel and disinfectant?"

He shook his head. "Worse than that. I haven't looked for anyone. I'm just waiting for you to come back, Emily. I don't want to break in another housekeeper."

"Housekeeper sounds like I answered the door for guests. I was the house *cleaner*. What happened between one Thursday afternoon and the next wasn't my worry. And I don't remember you exactly training me...."

He held up a hand. "The fact is I'm just going to wait 'til you feel like coming back. That's all."

"It's nice of you, David, but I'll understand if I lose the job. I lost my babysitting job with Melissa Singer. Can't be helped." But the truth was, although I would understand, I would be very upset if I lost that little job working for David. I'd had it since I was a kid and holding onto it for such a long time gave me a sense of pride. If only I could hold onto a boyfriend so well.

David cleared his throat. "Melissa's was a different situation. This isn't a little boy who needs constant supervision. This is a barely-lived-in house that could eventually use a good cleaning. It'll wait. In the meantime, I could maybe pick up some of the newspapers myself."

"Oh, man. Seriously? I don't even want to imagine what it looks like."

He chuckled. "No. That probably wouldn't be good for your recovery."

We arrived at the dining room and my table, laughing about David and his messy house. He pulled out my chair, and I slowly lowered myself into it and set Silver next to me. The other women at the table looked delighted about our visitor. I think one of them batted her eyelashes at David.

He smiled back and introduced himself, shaking hands all around. He turned back to me. "Emily, it was great to see you. I'm sorry we talked about my dirty house the whole time. I—well—I need to get to the airport. You take care, okay?"

"Sure. Yes, I will. Thanks for the visit, David." I lowered my voice and held my hand at the edge of my mouth so maybe not everyone would hear my next

MAGDALENA SCOTT

words. "And thanks for the flowers."

It shouldn't have been an awkward moment, saying goodbye for now to someone I'd known my whole life. A man whose family was so close to mine that he should have been in the 'older brother' category. I had more knowledge of David than many would—than perhaps his own siblings—since I'd had access to everything in his house for a dozen years. He looked down at me in the chair, and I imagined he wavered between the intent to kiss the top of my head as you might a child to a rash thought of kneeling down and giving me a big hug. Instead, he took my hand in both of his and, leaning down, whispered in my ear, "These ladies are all wondering what's up between us. Let's not ruin it for them entirely." He gently kissed my cheek and whispered, "Happy Thanksgiving."

"Happy Thanksgiving, David."

"And—do you mind if I come back to visit again? Maybe we can find another topic of discussion."

"Sounds nice," I said. I think he was gone before my blush was full-blown.

***

I was on my second trip through the halls, and exhausted, when Kim appeared. "Princess, was that the famous Adam who paid you a visit this morning?"

"What? Oh—no. Just a friend of the family. He's practically like a brother to me."

"Ah. Well, what a nice 'practically a brother' he seemed to be. Made quite a stir in the dining room, I heard."

"Yes. Well, he was just being silly. You never know what kind of mood David will be in. He's serious a lot of the time, but I think that's because his work gets him all keyed up. This morning he was on his way to the airport, so he wasn't 'at work' yet. By the time his work week is done, he'll arrive back home all stressed out." I stopped babbling, sorry I'd had more coffee than usual. Apparently, I couldn't handle my current level of caffeination. Kim didn't need to know David's routine or stress level or anything else about him.

She looked at me, waiting for me to say more, but I turned my face toward the walker and the floor and kept plodding.

"You're doing better, Princess. You're making progress."

"Isn't that the idea of me being here?"

"Yeah, but I wasn't sure you knew that. You seemed to think it was some kind of punishment or that people didn't want you to go home."

"Not true," I grumbled, remembering that's exactly

the way I had initially looked at rehab.

I took a few mores steps before realizing Kim wasn't walking beside me anymore. I stopped and glanced backward. She was just catching up with a teenage girl who was having a rough time learning how to steer her wheelchair. The girl, who looked frustrated enough to cry, began to grin shyly as soon as Kim talked to her. I turned back the way I had been going, glad to be alone with my thoughts instead of being chattered at the whole time.

Chapter Five

Turn the page, Emily.

I woke up to the words a few days after Thanksgiving. Knowing there wouldn't be anyone there, I still glanced around just in case. I was really tired of that stupid voice harping at me about something I didn't understand. I had come close to telling Steven, the counselor, that I kept hearing this sentence over and over, but figured it would only look bad for me, which I definitely did not need. So I kept it to myself, along with the dream I had that day I awakened at the hospital.

I pulled up to a sitting position, so I could see my Christmas tree better. Every time I looked at it, I remembered Dad and Mom bringing it in and Ben helping them decorate it because he'd been home for the long weekend. Dad had gotten kind of emotional telling how David and Jim Standish had refused payment when he went out to get a Christmas tree for the house as usual and also this little one for my room.

I was looking forward to lunch today because Gran and her BFF, Lillian Standish, were coming to the lockup to eat with me. This was kind of a big deal because it meant I got to sit at a different table instead of at my assigned place with the ladies whose conversations were always stuck in the past. I could never add anything, and they didn't want to talk about more current topics. We compromised in that they talked about their usual, and I ate in silence trying not to listen.

But at the lockup, when you had company at mealtime, you got special treatment because they didn't want the people paying the bills to know how miserable it was to live there. Yeah, I had it all figured out.

Lunch time had nearly arrived, and I was at the front door waiting when Gran and Lillian arrived, bearing a lush evergreen Christmas wreath Lillian had made at the tree farm's Christmas shop. They both hugged me and insisted we take the wreath to lunch with us as a centerpiece and hang it on the door of my room afterward.

"We had the nicest drive down here," Gran said, carrying the wreath.

"Yes," said Lillian, on the other side of me. "Beautiful day and we hit every traffic light green. You know what that means, Emily?"

"I don't think so."

"It means we'll hit every light red on the way back," said Gran. She nodded, believing it. "Oh well, we're not in as much of a hurry to get to Serendipity as we were to get here to see you." An aide showed us to the Special Table for Patient with Guest(s). Gran put the cheerful wreath in the center of the table, and the aide carried away the little centerpiece that was just like the ones on every other table.

I took a deep breath of the wreath's fresh pine scent. "It's amazing to think it's really the Christmas season."

Gran frowned. "I wish Thanksgiving could have been different for you, honey."

"It's okay. I understand that taking me home for a visit would have been a lot of extra driving and a big job for everybody. It was nice so much family came down to visit." My hands were in my lap and I laced my fingers together, concentrating on that and not on the scene of celebrating Thanksgiving at the lockup. It had felt so sad. Sure, my parents and siblings and Gran came for lunch, and Uncle Jamison and Aunt Darlene stopped by in the evening on their way to join the

Christmas shopping hysteria. In fact, it had been a big day for visitors, but that didn't make it a good day. This, though—having these ladies here now on a regular day made the place so much more bearable. I sighed, relaxing into conversation with women who'd known me my entire life but were never at a loss for topics to discuss. We touched on politics, books, movies, environmental issues, and somewhere during all the conversation, lunch was served, eaten, and cleared away. We were still sitting at our table when everyone else had gone, and one of the PTs came through the doorway heading toward me.

I had a sinking feeling when I saw the look on his face. "Uh oh. I bet I'm late for PT. I'll lose a sticker for this." I looked at the big clock and saw that I was very late.

"Hey, Leo. I'm so sorry. Time got away while we were talking." I made the introductions, and he was immediately charmed by both of the gracious ladies.

"Emily, I can see how that can happen, but you know we're on a schedule." Leo glanced at his watch which was the official time in his opinion—not any clock on any wall. "Okay, you've missed it entirely. I'll have to see what we can do to double schedule you or something." He nodded toward the ladies and said a gruff goodbye to me.

Gran shook her head, watching him walk away.

"Oh, Emily. I'm so sorry we got you in trouble."

"Gran, please don't apologize. It's my fault. I knew the schedule. I knew the schedule…" And I started to cry silent burning tears. "I'm so tired. I want to go home, Gran."

"Honey, honey." She slid her chair over next to mine and put her arm around me, nudged my head onto her shoulder.

Lillian slid her chair to the other side of mine and took my hand, rubbing it gently. "Emily, you're so much better. You're making progress, but you have to keep working with the people here. Try not to be negative, because they are making a wonderful difference for you. If you work *with* instead of *against* the therapists, I think you'll be surprised at the change that occurs."

"I'm not working against them." I sniffed and dug in my pocket for a tissue. "But maybe I could work a little harder. If it will get me out of here even five minutes sooner, it's worthwhile."

"Your parents are looking forward to having you home," Gran said. "These weeks have been hard on them."

I so badly did not want to make that regression. "I can't go back to their house."

Gran looked at me sternly with that no-nonsense look of hers that could stop a truck. "You'll break their hearts if you don't, Emily. They've done everything to help you get better. The least you can do for them is go there when you're released."

I knew she was right and that I would have to worry later about gaining my independence. "Okay." I sniffed. "Okay...."

Gran stood. "We'll go with you to your room now and put your wreath up. We need to get back to Serendipity. Lillian has to go to work, and I'm hosting bridge club tonight." Yep, these two ladies had more going on in their lives than I did by a long shot.

Silver and I walked with them to my room. They hung the wreath, and I accompanied them to the front door. It was more steps than I was scheduled for, but I needed it. As they drove away, Kim bounced around the corner, up the front sidewalk, and through the entryway.

"Hey, Princess. Shouldn't you be in PT?"

How irritating for her to notice. "Close, but you missed the time. Unfortunately, so did I. Got in some trouble for insubordination too. It's twenty lashes at sunset for me."

Kim shook her head. "Girl, how'd you miss it? Not

like it's hard to look at a schedule."

"My grandmother and her friend were here for lunch, and I just lost track of time. As I said, I've been duly reamed."

"It's good to know somebody gives you grief when I'm not here to administer it." Kim passed me and walked toward the employee's lounge.

"Hey," I called after her. "What are you doing here at this time of day? Don't you usually work first shift?"

"Mostly first. Some seconds, some thirds. It's all good—I can use the money. Gotta clock in, Princess, or I'll be late too. Catch you later when I come to read your bedtime story, tuck you in, and shine up that tiara." She shot me one of those crazy-bright smiles and ducked into the lounge.

After that, I noticed Kim was at Meadowbrooke at all hours. She'd pull first, second, and third shifts all in the same week. I couldn't imagine how she was able to keep going, let alone get any decent sleep when she wasn't on a set schedule. Yet, she was always laughing and teasing people and seemed to cheer up most of the residents and staff, as well. It was amazing to be sitting in the dining room with nothing particular going on— just a bunch of inmates with our gruel, as it were—and in would walk Kim with that big, bright smile. She'd stop to joke with someone here and there as she made her way through the room, maybe just a round-trip to the kitchen to get a glass of iced tea for somebody. Next, she'd work her way back doing the same, and by this time, if you'd had some kind of a scale to measure happiness, it would have gone from about 1.0 to 8.5. It was super impressive to me, despite the fact an 8.5 wouldn't get you a gold medal if Making People Happy was an Olympic event.

Yep, Always Cheerful Kim had gone from being irritating, to extremely irritating, to intriguing.

One day, when she was in my room, I blurted it out. "What's with you, Kim? How can you come in here at all hours and work, doing—pardon my saying it—some pretty menial stuff—and always be happy?"

"Who told you I'm always happy?"

"Well…nobody had to tell me. I can see it on your face, of course. And the way you talk to everybody, even if a person was blind they'd know you were smiling because of the tone of your voice."

"And they'd know from the tone of your voice that you're always frowning, Emily. Why are you so unhappy?"

I glared at her, undeterred. "I asked first."

"So you did." She finished straightening my bed, winked at me, and left.

Chapter Six

Karly and Danielle were hanging out with me in a sitting area one evening. They had plucked a couple of board games off a shelf in the rec room, but none of us was in the mood to play after all. Kim went past, pushing an inmate in a wheelchair, chattering happily the whole time. The inmate was taken in, as all of them were, by her cheerful banter. Laughter followed in their wake.

"I wonder what's up with Always Cheerful Kim," I muttered.

"Who? The aide?" Karly watched them go down the hall.

"Yeah. Look at her. She's like that all the time, and she's working some crazy hours. How can she be that way?"

"Maybe she's on something," Danielle offered helpfully, putting away the last board game and stacking the boxes on the table between us. She leaned on them to stare after Kim and her charge.

I pushed away from the table and slowly got up, needing to move before my leg started to feel stiff. "I guess that's possible. Something's definitely not right with her."

"So find out what it is, Emily," said Karly. "That'd be more entertaining than sitting here playing board games or watching TV."

"Right. But how?" I started walking. Karly and Danielle stood and fell into slow step on either side of me as good old Silver led the way.

"You know, I bet this place is like Serendipity," Danielle suggested. "Everybody knows everybody, right? You could probably find out a lot about Kim if you just asked around." She shrugged. "It's something to do. She is kind of a mystery, isn't she? Maybe she was actually sent here from the hospital in order to spy on you." She snapped her fingers, looking pleased with herself. "Oooh. Maybe Dr. Jay hired Kim to do patient follow-up espionage."

"She may be the star of a new reality show," said Karly. "Undercover Aide. What d'you think? You could become famous as the person who reveals what she's really up to."

Of course, it wouldn't be anything interesting like that, but I still wanted to understand Kim better.

The next time I was in a physical therapy session with Leo, I decided to give it a shot. Leo was a big guy, bodybuilder for decades I'd guess, and probably close to fifty years old. He had photos of his wife, kids, and grandkids on his desk, and it seemed he had a new one to show off every time I went for a session. Unless you missed a session with him, Leo was a very friendly, easy-going guy, so I figured he would either share information or, at least, not be obnoxious about my asking.

"So, Leo, you know Kim, the aide who walked up here with me?"

"Sure. She's a good kid."

"No, I mean do you really know her? Like, her family and stuff? Past employment?"

Leo's heavy brows knit. "What's on your mind, Emily?"

"I just wondered. It's a simple question."

"I'd suggest if you want to know more about Kim, you talk to her, not to me or anyone else who works here."

I crossed my arms and waited while Leo wrote something on a chart. That's the response I got from everyone I asked, employee and inmate alike. I can only guess none of them had grown up in a small town where, if you wanted to know something about someone, you asked their neighbor or co-worker. Or you eavesdropped when the person walked away to hear what the people she'd just been talking to would say when she stepped away from the group and was out of earshot. Asking someone directly was just not done.

Gran came in to visit one day when I had failed in another attempt to get information about Kim. I had just struck out again, and in frustration, smacked the heel of my hand on my walker hard enough that I expected I had bruised it. My hand, that is.

"Emily Elizabeth, you stop that right now."

"Oh—hi, Gran. What? What did I do?"

"I'm not certain but, young lady, I know a temper tantrum when I see one."

My shoulders sagged. "I'm just exasperated about that aide who's so cheerful. She's driving me crazy."

Gran sat down on a side chair in my room. "Oh—Kim? She's sweet. Such an encourager to everyone too."

"Yeah." I looked around and lowered my voice.

"Doesn't it seem way over the top to you?"

"Not at all. I think she's quite sincere. If I had to guess, I'd say she's overcome some great difficulty or sorrow."

"Whoa—the girl who's always blinding everyone with her smile?"

"Have you ever noticed, Emily, that people who have an easy life tend to take it for granted and those who struggle and overcome usually have a very positive attitude?"

"No—are we still talking about Kim?"

Gran's eyes twinkled. "Of course, we are, honey. You're the one who brought up the topic, remember?"

Chapter Seven

One day during lunch, a man in an expensive looking suit and a woman in a classic black dress entered the dining room, talking in low tones with the facility administrator, Ms. Sullivan. A janitor wheeled in some media equipment and set up the portable public address system that was used for special events. No one else seemed to know what was going on, and there was lots of murmuring throughout the dining room.

Once the sound check was done, Ms. Sullivan stepped up to the microphone and introduced our two guests. "Mr. and Mrs. Chambers are here to award a plaque and documentation to the winner of the nursing scholarship they have endowed. Beginning with the next semester, a full scholarship to nursing school has been awarded to our own Kimberly Rose."

Beaming, she turned and held out one hand toward

the far wall. I looked in the direction she was gesturing, and there was Always Cheerful Kim, her features changed completely from the usual. At first, I thought she was frowning but realized she was crying. Evidently, our Kim was Kimberly Rose. I was struck by the fact I'd never taken the time to learn her last name.

Everyone started congratulating her, and it took a while before she could make her way through the giddy inmates to claim the plaque and large white envelope. There were a couple of false starts before her voice was steady enough to make her little acceptance speech.

"Wow. When I applied for the Chambers Nursing Scholarship, I definitely didn't expect to get it. But some of my friends here and at the hospital pushed me into trying anyway." She cleared her throat and her big smile, a touch wobbly, reappeared—directed this time at her benefactors. "This is a dream come true for me, Mr. and Mrs. Chambers."

Mrs. Chambers gave Kim a big hug, and Mr. Chambers put a fatherly arm around her shoulders while his wife stood at the microphone. "Each year we award this scholarship to a person who has shown outstanding character and desire to serve others through a career in nursing. Besides going over each application, we also interview three references for each applicant. Ms. Rose's own story as a breast cancer survivor after losing her mother to that terrible disease and her selfless dedication to her patients made this year's selection process easier than it sometimes is. My husband and I feel honored to play a part in educating a wonderful new nurse."

That's when the crowd, as they say, went wild. Residents of varying ambulatory capacity wanted to give Kim a big hug. There was so much happiness and picture-taking that my own jaws began to ache in sympathy. Finally, I grabbed Silver and headed to my room and relative quiet. I had wanted more information about Kim and today's speeches had offered some. She came into my room a while later, doing her usual straightening once-over.

"Congratulations on the scholarship, Kim. Full ride—that's really something."

She stopped bustling for a moment. "Thanks, Princess. I really didn't expect to get it."

"Sounds like Mr. and Mrs. Chambers are in your cheering section now. That won't hurt either."

She shook her head. "Seems unreal, to be honest."

"I've never understood why you seem happy all the time. Now from what they said, I mean, about losing your mom and you having survived breast cancer..." I let my voice trail off, uncertain how to phrase what I needed to find out. "I just don't get it. Sounds like your life has been really rough, and I know your work schedule has been horrible lately, yet you're always so upbeat. *How?*"

She considered my question for a moment, expelling a long breath as she lowered herself to a chair. "Emily, every time I wake up, I'm grateful for another day of life. Another chance to see the sun or feel the rain on my face. Another chance to make a difference for someone. There are times, especially near Mom's birthday or the anniversary of the day she died, I have to dig down deep to find a bit of happiness I can share with others. It's what I do, to help others cope with their situations."

In spite of myself I pictured my first interaction with Kim when she was getting me ready for my first hop from bed to chair, trying to lighten the mood with references to *The Princess Bride*. I had been horribly rude to her then and plenty of times since. Had I slammed her on a day she'd been particularly missing her mother?

Kim leaned a little forward in the chair, her face passionate. "Back when I was going to treatments, I would have loved to have had a nurse aide tell me a couple of stupid jokes to cheer me up for a minute. Just a minute, you know, when you're not thinking about pain or death, but laughing and normal like you used to be." Her voice broke, and she swallowed hard.

Touched by her sudden openness, I watched in fascination as Always Cheerful Kim allowed her façade to drop. I'd never given a moment's thought to her emotional well-being, yet she was always selflessly trying to improve mine and that of everyone else she worked with.

She shook her head, perhaps to get her emotions under control. "It's not a lot of effort for me to wear a smile, when I know what a difference it can make for a patient. And now I'll get to do even more. A nurse!" Her face shone with happiness. "I'll touch so many lives and be a liaison between some doctors with their patients. There are times that doctors and patients don't understand each other very well."

I remembered the day at the hospital when I told my parents about Dr. Jay's visit and Mom's quick exit to the nurses' station. Dad said the nurses had always helped explain what was going on with me. It was clear my parents had found comfort in being able to confer with a nurse when they needed to, since doctors tended to be there and gone before you realized you wanted to ask a question.

Kim brushed away a renegade tear and stood up to leave. "I don't understand you, Emily. You've been allowed a second chance too, but you don't even seem glad about it. So many who have lost their lives would have been glad to be where you are right now."

That pulled me out of my reverie. "Of course, I'm glad to be alive. You don't know anything about me, Kim. Don't be so quick to judge." I groaned inwardly at my ugly tone.

She raised a brow. "Hmm. Maybe. I think you take a lot for granted. Your family. Having a home to go back to when you leave here."

Not the home I had intended to return to—the one with Adam. "You're making it sound perfect. I don't have a boyfriend anymore, remember. He lost interest since my wreck."

Kim shrugged. "Men. Who can figure them? My boyfriend left when I got the cancer diagnosis and was never heard from again. I realize now it's better this way because he was so needy and self-centered. If he'd stayed around, I'd have been babying him in spite of being unable to take care of myself. That's the kind of relationship we had. We were both childish and self-absorbed." Her face changed briefly, and she winked at me. "I will say he was handsome, smart, funny, and a great kisser."

"But a loser."

She nodded. "Yes. Relationship-wise anyway. He has a responsible job and makes good money."

But he ran out on her and didn't help support her

through her cancer treatments? What a complete rat.

I wished for a way to ease the remaining pain, but all I could think of was to help dis men. "I can relate a little bit, Kim. In spite of his good traits, which I've mostly forgotten, my boyfriend, Adam was always finding fault with whatever I did. At first when he didn't come to the hospital, or here, I was hurt by it. But I've gotten used to him not being around. Now that I think about it, I can imagine if he did visit, he'd be telling me I wasn't healing fast enough or that I was using the walker wrong." I couldn't help smiling, picturing that. Then I patted my thigh. "Without a doubt, he'd be pointing out that I've gained some weight since the wreck." Yep. If Adam was still in my life, he would have been complicating it. I didn't need that. And I didn't need him.

"Good for you, Princess. That's a step toward being the best version of yourself. Realizing that you're complete without an 'other half.' I've become a stronger and better person since being on my own again."

Their relationship sounded very similar to mine and Adam's. He and I had been so focused on our own self-interests, it's a surprise we had ever taken time to be in each other's lives at all. No wonder our breakup hadn't been a surprise to Karly or Danielle. I imagine I was the only one surprised by it.

"One thing, Princess. I was eventually able to forgive him. It was wrenching to do that, because feeding my hurt and anger had become almost a hobby for me. But, finally, I realized being angry didn't hurt him but was just another burden for me to carry. Just something to keep in mind." Kim looked at her watch. "Hey, I gotta get a move on. Later, Princess!"

The nickname, which had been mildly irritating at first, didn't bother me anymore. I'd always known she used it because she considered me spoiled. But now I understood part of why she thought of me that way—and how very right she was.

I spent a lot of the rest of that day thinking about my conversation with Kim. She had been through her own personal hell but had come out on the other side stronger and more positive because of how she had chosen to process it. It wasn't lost on me that I was at a crossroads in my own life. Everything now seemed to be easily separated under two headings: *Before the Wreck* or *After the Wreck*. The *Before* Emily wasn't someone I wanted to spend time with anymore. That Emily was a bit like the pre-diagnosis Kim—childish and self-absorbed. I could look back now with shame at ways I had behaved toward my family, Adam, or my string of many previous boyfriends.

Had there been multiple boyfriends because they had treated me badly and moved on, or had I been so wrapped up in myself that a healthy relationship couldn't possibly flourish? Thinking about it carefully now for the first time in my life, I knew it was mostly the latter.

***

Now that I was getting to know Kim, I looked forward to talking to her again. Which, of course, meant it seemed like ages before she worked another shift. Finally, I caught a glimpse of her sailing down the hallway, as I was sitting with Karly and Danielle in the rec room not playing board games again.

"Hey, there's Kim." I got up with Silver as quickly as I could manage and started in the direction she had gone.

"Kim who?" Karly and Danielle were immediately on either side of me as I made snail's pace progress.

"You know. Kim Rose, the nurse aide."

"Oh. I don't think I knew her last name."

"No, you didn't. But now you know. She won a full-ride nursing scholarship. Isn't that amazing?"

"Wow. Yeah, it sure is. Tell me again why we're slowly chasing her?"

"I just want to talk to her. We had a conversation

the other day that we didn't get to finish."

"A conversation? Not just jabbing at each other with one-liners?" asked Danielle.

"Come on. That's kids' stuff."

"Oh. My mistake." Danielle fell back and so did Karly. I didn't worry about that since, of course, they could catch up as quickly as they wanted. Eventually, I realized why they weren't walking anymore. The door Kim had gone through said *Staff Only*. I stopped short, staring at the words—large red letters on a white background. Surely, she would come out soon.

Twenty minutes later, Karly finally stopped pacing. "Okay, I'm going home if our whole visit is going to consist of standing or pacing outside this door."

"We could knock on it," I offered.

"Emily, that's weird," said Danielle. "She's in an employee lounge having a meeting or something. It's a work thing, and this is where she works. If you want to talk to her, I bet you can tell someone to put a note in a mailbox for her or something. Anyway, how come you have this sudden obsession with a nurse aide you've always disliked?"

"I haven't always disliked her."

"Yes, you have. You told us the story yourself.

You took one look at her that first day she was going to help you walk and knew she was the enemy. Oh, how did you put it? You 'knew her purpose was to torture you.'" Danielle smiled at the dramatic turn of phrase. "Sound familiar?"

"Well, if I said that, I was wrong."

Karly struck an attitude pose with one hand on her hip, something I remembered doing myself many times. "So she wasn't intent on torturing you there or transferred here for more of the same?"

"Of course not," I huffed. "She had to get a second job, and Meadowbrooke was hiring. Kim's had a hard time the last few years." I wasn't sure if I was supposed to relate the story of her fight with cancer and losing her Mom. "She has bills to pay, so of course she had to get a second job. I really respect her for doing that. I'm surprised at you girls for being so narrow-minded."

Karly and Danielle looked at each other, blinked, and looked back at me.

"Sorry," said Danielle. "We didn't know you and Kim had...bonded."

I searched her face but couldn't tell if she was being serious or sarcastic.

"Kim is not the person I thought she was." I turned and headed back the way we had come.

"You originally thought she was—what?" Danielle prodded.

This conversation was my own fault, and I mentally kicked myself for starting it. Physically kicking myself was out of the question unless I wanted to start over totally on my rehab.

"Um. I don't know. I think I had this perception she had an easy life with nothing to do but poke at me when she was at work and buy lots of toothpaste for that...somewhat irritating...smile of hers. Does that make sense?"

They both nodded. "Yes, for you," said Danielle. "And she does come on pretty strong in the cheerfulness department."

"Turns out that's sincere. She's had some hard times, and after she got through those, she was grateful to be alive. Not bitter about what had gone on, if you know what I mean."

"Yeah. I know some people who are bitter," said Danielle. "Not pleasant for anybody involved." She shot Karly a look that I don't think I was supposed to see.

"Hey, girls, sorry for the sudden Meaning of Life conversation. Must be something in the water around here." We laughed, and I was glad when Karly changed the topic to an in-depth review of the new manicure place in Serendipity. She showed off her nails, which were gorgeously gelled and blinged. Not that the girls couldn't carry on a serious discussion, but they had driven to Meadowbrooke to cheer me up. I decided to let them do it, and the rest of our visit was total fluff.

Even if Kim had walked up to us at that point, I knew I couldn't talk to her about the topics I had on my mind. Not with the girls standing there. Kim and I had something in common that even my best friends couldn't fully understand, because—thank God—neither of them had had a close brush with death. I knew I could learn a lot from Kim if I spent more time with her.

According to Leo, I was progressing pretty well on my physical therapy, so I might be able to leave Meadowbrooke in a couple of weeks. Never in my life had I realized I didn't have any time to waste. I had Kim to thank for that.

***

Kim walked in wearing the megawatt smile that meant something entirely different to me these days. Instead of bustling around, she walked over to the table and gently touched a daisy petal and sighed silently. "Hey. Nice flowers. That David of yours is very thoughtful."

"He's not *my* David. He's just a friend of the family."

Kim arched a brow, but nodded. "Okay, if that's how you want to see him. Very thoughtful friend of the family."

"Come on. It's not like this is the first bouquet of flowers I've had since I got here." I regretted saying that because it sounded like boasting.

"Ah. Good point. Your parents have brought some and those two girlfriends of yours. And didn't your sisters bring you a handful of hemlock one day?" She touched a finger to her chin, pretending to struggle with her memory.

"No, the twins haven't brought me flowers or even deadly foliage. However, I think you have to do more than be in the room with hemlock for it to kill you." I laughed. "Those two are awful. Thanks for noticing."

She shook her head. "Difficult not to. I guess they're at the worst possible age."

"That's what I keep telling myself. Surely, they will eventually become human. Maybe another couple of years. My poor mom."

Kim hopped into the deep window sill, more agile than I'd have expected, given her size. "Why do you say that?"

"Well, Mom is the old-fashioned kind. She's always stayed at home and raised kids. The twins graduate from high school in the spring, and God willing, they're off to college in the fall. The house will be quiet. Mom deserves a good rest after hassling with those two plus my wreck thrown into the mix. My brother Ben is the only bright spot right now."

"And your dad."

"Well, yes. Sure. You don't have to remind me. Dad is great. He's supportive of all of us. He's done his share of cheering at ball games, chaperoning dances. The usual chores for parents of active kids. But you know, he works a lot. So the biggest part of parenting has been on Mom."

"What will she do when she's home alone?"

"I have no idea. The thought hadn't even occurred to me."

"I bet it has to her."

"Probably. Wow! Life will be completely different for her. But in a good way." *I hope.* I pictured Mom in that big house all day with nothing major going wrong with any of us kids. All she would have to do is cook for her and Dad and clean the house which would take next to no time with just two of them living in it. Maybe she would get a job or do more volunteer work.

Her PTA days would be over, but she could volunteer somewhere else. It was weird to think of Mom being at loose ends for hours every day.

"When you leave here, are you going to live with your parents?"

"I don't want to because it feels like taking a step backward." I smiled. "But I'm lucky to take any step at all, right? So, yeah, if they'll have me, that's where I'm headed."

"Might be about time to decide for sure, Princess. Word on the street is that your days at Meadowbrooke are numbered."

I looked past her out the window. "That's great news. I didn't want to come here in the first place, but now I'm glad I did. If I hadn't, well, I would have been a horrible burden on my family because I couldn't do anything on my own. But besides healing somewhat and becoming physically stronger, I think—I hope—I'll leave here a better person than when I arrived." I couldn't put into words how important she had been in that change.

"I'll miss our little sniping sessions, Princess. No kidding." She looked again at the vase of daisies. "I hope you'll let me know how your relationship progresses with *David-only-a-friend-of-the-family*. If you send me a wedding invitation, I'll wear a dress and everything."

My face grew hot with an embarrassed blush, but I refused to take her joke seriously. "What? Go somewhere in something other than scrubs? I don't know, Kim. That sounds radical."

"I'm okay with doing something radical for a friend."

"Oh."

She smiled at me, and at that moment I understood how the Grinch felt when his heart grew three sizes in one day. "It's been a long time since I made a new friend," I said. "The way I've treated you, especially at first...well, I probably don't deserve your friendship."

Kim shrugged and slid off the window ledge, adjusted her scrub top so it hung straight as possible over her hips. "It isn't about deserving. I'm giving you my friendship, Princess. You decide what to do with it. I think we'll be okay." She checked her watch. "Gotta run now. You'd better get some laps in before the next meal. That might earn you some brownie points. Plus it's a good idea to keep pushing yourself every day. Right?" She waggled her fingers at me. "Later."

I don't know what I had expected to discuss with Kim, but it sure wasn't Mom's potential time management issues after the twins graduated high school. I felt let down that she always challenged me on my point of view about something and never spent time praising me for my progress here. I told myself it was just her nature to always push people while helping them enjoy doing their best. Getting to my feet for a lap, I took a step to touch one of the daisy petals as she had done. So soft, so lovely. I was grateful for David's thoughtfulness and chuckled to myself at Kim's idea that he was romantically interested in me.

Because we'd been discussing him, there was a little flutter of excitement in my stomach when David came in to see me the next day, finding me returning to my room after rehab with Leo. I was exhausted and sore.

"Emily?"

I turned around and saw him, dressed down in jeans and boots and a Carhartt jacket over a dark T-shirt. No serious businessman attire for him from Thanksgiving to Christmas when he was a full-time employee of the Standish Family Christmas Tree Farm. It was so unfair for David to look even yummier today than when he'd arrived all dressed up. Unfair because as I'd said to Kim, he was, and always would be, just a friend.

I gulped and shook my head at him as he walked toward me with the bouquet. "David Standish, you are ruining my reputation around here."

"Oh? How's that?"

"You know—the daisies. And you coming to visit, looking all handsome and…well, a little scruffy now that your tree-season beard is coming in. Finally, everybody has stopped pitying me that Adam chose my wreck as an easy way out of our relationship." I felt strong for being able to joke about it. "Yeah, now they think—" I leaned closer to speak more softly. "—there's something going on between you and me. Entirely your fault."

"Oh, wow. I'm sorry. Did you want to be an object of pity?"

"Ouch. Yes, to be honest, I did want that, at first." I shook my head, remembering. "I was just teasing, David. I love the flowers. It's really sweet of you."

He rolled his eyes. "Not so sweet. I have an ulterior motive."

"You're fiendishly cornering the daisy market?"

"Shhh." He looked around covertly. "Don't blurt it out, for goodness sake. Well, you guessed part of it. There's the daisy market, plus this gives me an excuse to check on you—your progress, that is. I like knowing how you're getting along. I like seeing the color back in your cheeks and watching you get around on your own with a little less effort each time. Pretty impressive, my dear. Gives me hope that my house will eventually be cleaned."

I swatted at him with one hand without even a bit of unsteadiness. I was leaning much less on Silver now and was pleased with that. David rubbed the place on his arm where I'd managed to tap him. The muscle was nice and solid. I had a flash of wanting those strong arms around me but blinked it away.

"Mind if I walk with you? I'll put the flowers in your room and toss the old ones."

"The others are still pretty, but they'll be glad to have company. And so am I." My face grew warm, and I wondered how evident it was to him that I was feeling more than friendship. "Please do walk with me. Do you have much time?"

"Some. I got the evening off for good behavior. Dean Williams is helping at the farm this evening, and since it's Monday, it shouldn't be crazy busy. Did you know it's Monday, or are you so busy rehabbing that you lose track of the days?"

"Oh. I knew it, but I'd forgotten. When you don't go anywhere, one day is pretty much like the next. It surprises me you're free for the evening. Isn't that kind of a big deal for you this time of year?"

"Yep." He paused and seemed to come to a

decision. "Would you like to go for a drive?"

"What? Oh, I'd love a drive. It's sunny out today, isn't it?"

"It was. Nearly dusk now, but the air is warmer than it should be this time of year. Who do I have to talk to in order to bust you out of here for an hour or two?"

Excitement bubbled up inside me as I walked along trying to act normal. A trip in a car, going nowhere, just because we had decided to do it. That was a simple pleasure I had taken for granted my entire life.

We delivered the flowers to my room and set them next to the older ones, and David rifled through my closet for a jacket.

"You don't have anything warm in here. Don't you go out?"

"Actually, no. It's…a little complicated. Maybe you'll want to skip it."

He shook his head. "No chance. You can wear my jacket if you like." He slipped off his big farm jacket and tucked it into the crook of his arm. "It's not your size but more appropriate than just a bathrobe."

I'd wear a blanket and call it a mink coat, if it meant going out. "I feel like a little kid getting to ride in her daddy's new car for the first time."

"Let's not get the age difference blown out of proportion again, Emily."

And yet, when I realized the ten years separating us wasn't insurmountable, my mind wanted to take us away from friendship, toward something more romantic. That was probably a waste of energy and might lead to disappointment down the road.

We made the right arrangements with the right people, and at the front door I took a deep, steadying breath.

"See my car?" He pointed out into the lot at his silver BMW. "Think you want to walk that far, or should I drive it up here to the loading zone?"

"I can walk it." David helped me get my arms into his jacket and I buttoned it, but it was big and loose. The breeze made it billow as I walked. "Look at me— I'm a parade inflatable."

David laughed. A beautiful sunset was beginning to gather. I stood for a moment and reveled in the colors then noticed the building's layout for the first time ever.

"You know, I didn't even realize that direction was west until this moment. I haven't paid a lot of attention to sunrises and sunsets." I looked over my shoulder at Meadowbrooke. "I guess the window of my room faces north, so that makes sense." I had been so wrapped up in myself, I was out of touch with the outside world.

Getting into the car wasn't pretty, but it wasn't a disaster either. That's a skill Leo had me working on now, and I could appreciate how much further I had to go before I mastered it. After David stowed the walker behind my seat, I had a moment to inhale the scent of his familiar aftershave before he hopped in to drive.

"It's not ballet, but you've got some interesting moves going there, Emily." David's teasing kept me from being embarrassed about my awkwardness. He put on a pair of sunglasses and started the powerful engine. Meadowbrooke shrank away in the rearview mirror.

"I've been trying to perfect a new method of getting in and out of cars. Wait 'til you see the dismount, mister. You're gonna be in awe."

He laughed. "I can hardly wait." He stopped at the street and gestured at the option of turning left or right. "Which direction?"

That feeling in my chest again, of my heart feeling differently than it ever had before. This was an overwhelmingly strong sense of gratitude. "Could we go somewhere to watch the river for a few minutes?"

David flipped the left turn indicator and pulled onto the street. "Great idea. Kentucky side, so we can see the sun go down?"

"Awesome." I sank into the soft leather seat, watching houses and businesses flash past. When we stopped at a light, sometimes people ogled the shiny BMW, and David, then the car again. I imagined their thought process. Handsome, successful guy is taking his disheveled kid sister somewhere to drop her off. I looked down at his jacket that I was still wearing, inhaled his scent and couldn't have cared less about anyone's opinion of my appearance. Even if I looked like a messed-up kid sister, I was a happy one.

"David, could we have music? All my CD's and my radio are packed away somewhere. I'm really tired of the music that's piped in at Meadowbrooke."

"Hey, sure thing." He turned on the stereo and a solo by Kenny G lilted through the air. Before long, we crossed the Ohio River into Louisville and parked riverside, looking west.

"Flip that visor down if it's too bright for you, Emily."

"No, that's okay. It's wonderful." I squinted because it actually was almost overwhelming, but before long the sun had dropped another degree and the Indiana skyline was bathed in shades of orange, red, and, inexplicably, gray-blue. David had left the music playing.

"I love your Kenny G collection."

"Oh?"

"Um—yep. Sometimes when I'm cleaning, I listen to music. Actually, all the time. I like his stuff even though he's old."

David pulled a face. "Everybody seems old to you." He turned his head away from me back to the sunset. "I'm glad you're okay with Kenny. This is my second copy of his *Paradise* CD. I totally wore out the first one. I have a few other CDs in here, and, of course, satellite radio. But there's something reassuring about knowing what song is going to play next."

I nodded. "No kidding. There's not much you can count on in life. It's nice to at least know what song's coming up. I like predictable sometimes."

"That surprises me, Emily."

"Does it? Why?"

"You seem to have spent your life going for the unexpected."

Had I? "Huh. Well, sometimes that works out and sometimes it blows up in your face. I mean, I don't want a boring life, but a little stability at this point might be nice."

"You have your family. That's stability."

"Yes, I do, and I'm lucky to have them. I don't know where I'd be if they weren't willing to cart me home like their little girl and take care of me."

He looked at me and grimaced. "Hardly like a little girl. They're just making sure you get a fresh start."

"That's what I need, for sure. I'm starting over from scratch. I'm working on being a whole new Emily."

He turned back away again, watching the sunset. The slight movement sent a new hint of his aftershave wafting toward me. I caught myself licking my lips.

"That sounds drastic."

Back into the conversation, "new Emily." "It is, I guess. I could have lived better up to this point, but I can't change that. I can only move on from here." I absently fingered the coarse fabric of his jacket and surreptitiously gave it another little sniff. "Poor Mom and Dad. They've made plenty of good suggestions to us over the years, most of which my sisters and I have ignored. But not Ben. Ben was always the perfect child."

"And that's a bad thing?" A corner of David's mouth turned upward.

"Oh no. No. Sorry—that came out wrong. I'm crazy about my brother. I'm glad that somehow he was smart enough to listen at the right times and rebel when nothing awful came of it. Wish I'd lived that way more."

"Do you, Emily? If you could go back a year or more, would you do things differently?"

I turned fully toward the sunset now, giving it my rapt attention. "Well, sure. Wouldn't everybody, given the chance?" There were dozens of things I wished I'd done differently. I heard him shrug, the movement of his muscles in the long-sleeve T-shirt slipping along the leather seat.

"I don't know that I would change much," he said. "Maybe install a built-in vacuum system in my house."

I laughed, relieved as the serious tone of the conversation faded. "You seem to think a lot about cleaning your house."

"Not really. I think a lot these days about *you* cleaning it—or whether you won't do that anymore." I heard him turn toward me and saw the movement in my peripheral vision. "I'm relieved that you're so well, Emily. We thought we might be saying good-bye to you forever."

Cautiously, I dragged my eyes from the sunset,

which was just a glimmer now, to look at David. His eyes had a haunted look. Surely, that had been there before, and I had failed to notice. Surely, this turn of conversation hadn't caused an appearance of emotional distress.

"I'm glad that didn't happen. Me dying, I mean. And I'm super thankful that rehab is going so well. I don't deserve it, you know. The progress. I didn't want to go to Meadowbrooke, and I made a big fuss about it to Mom and Dad. I know they just want to do what's best for me. I've always been too concerned about myself to care how anything I said or did affected my family."

"Seems you're growing up all of a sudden, Emily."

"About time too. I almost missed my chance to do it. Almost left this earth." I stopped and nearly chose not to explain but decided I wanted to tell him. "I was at the edge of it, David. I know I was. I had this amazing vision, or dream, of—anyway, I'm sure I was at the point of passing over to the other side." My throat tightened. "But it wasn't scary. It was pretty and so peaceful." The scene scrolled through my memory. "And suddenly I wasn't there anymore. I was in the hospital bed with tubes in me, and Mom was leaning on the bed looking miserable."

"I have no doubt your mom was miserable. Seeing you lie there was torture."

"Oh. Were you there? In the hospital, I mean, when I was unconscious?"

"Yes. Lots of people were there, not that everyone went into the room with you. People drove down to be supportive of your parents. Sit with them in the waiting room or whatever." He took off his sunglasses and perched them on his head. "My mom took a supply of chocolate chip cookies more than once, so Jennifer would have something to offer visitors. Both of our mothers are such hostesses, aren't they?"

"Wow. That's weird but cool. Very nice of Lillian."

"We all react to life's challenges in different ways. Mom's main reaction is food of one kind or another, but mainly cookies." He shrugged. "Who's to say it isn't the best method to help people who are going through hard times?"

"Yours is flowers."

"What? My what is flowers?"

"Your method. You've been bringing me flowers."

"Yes."

"So, that's what you usually do when you visit someone who is hurt or sick. Take flowers. It's really nice. Gran does that too."

David didn't reply but looked out across the river. What had I said to derail the conversation?

He started the car and Kenny G faded a bit. "What now? Do you want to go somewhere else, look at different scenery?"

"I don't know. Now that it's getting dark, there's not as much scenery visible."

He sighed, turning toward me, but managed a crooked grin. "Quick lap around the big city? Get some dinner?"

"Hey, we could, couldn't we? My first non-institutional food in a long while. Sounds amazing."

We chose a local seafood restaurant on the Indiana side of the river and ate carryout at a picnic table. It was cold but such a thrill to be outdoors breathing fresh air.

"You're going to have frostbite on those hands by the time we get you back to Meadowbrooke." He paused, watching me cradle the paper cup of steaming coffee. "They'll never let me borrow you again if I return you in damaged condition."

"I started this outing in damaged condition. Besides, you're the one not wearing a coat." I set the cup down and took another bite of the delicious fish sandwich, followed it with a fork full of cole slaw. "The coffee helps. I don't know how you can sit there and drink iced tea and not be frozen."

He leaned an elbow on the table, the picture of relaxation. "Mind over matter, Emily. I choose to believe I'm comfortably warm, so I am. You should try it sometime."

"Maybe. I've got some mind over *leg* to work out before I move on to frostbite denial."

"Okay. I'll give you a pass."

"And your jacket."

He chuckled, gesturing toward me with his plastic fork. "No, the jacket is a loaner."

"Wow. That's low. And here I thought you were a good guy. But I guess just because you bring a girl flowers—" I didn't say anything more because I was riveted in place as David stood, leaned across the table and kissed me. His action took me completely by surprise, because I'd never sensed any hint of a romantic feeling from him. And it was a gentle, brief kiss. By the time I realized I wanted to kiss him back, it was over. His hand, which had momentarily caressed my face, was gone too, and I suddenly felt colder.

He pushed his food packaging away and crossed his arms on the table, shaking his head slowly. "Probably shouldn't have done that."

"Oh. Why not?"

"You probably didn't want me to."

Could I tell him the truth—that the possibility of a kiss from him hadn't even occurred to me, but a second one seemed like a great idea? Instead, I carefully stood up, balanced myself with both palms on the tabletop, and got as close to kissing him as I could manage without toppling over. I wasn't going to let this moment pass without any input from me.

And it was worth the risk. I didn't get there and have my lips hanging out in the breeze without a warm reception. Oh no, not at all. David not only closed the distance and kissed me back, he stood and supported me by my upper arms so I wasn't in danger of falling. It might have been the most awkward effort toward a kiss in the history of the world, but the results were amazing. This is what a kiss was supposed to feel like, I realized. Compared to this, every other kiss in my life had been lacking. Who knew? He was strong, gentle, and passionate, yet not pushy. I was amazed to learn that a kiss from this man was better than anything with anyone had ever been. In the romance novels, a kiss that's so much better than any other is a sign of true love.

True love with David Standish? *Nah.* He was just really, really experienced. I'd seen plenty of proof over the years when cleaning his house.

One of the little cardboard food containers was picked up by a gust of wind, and the kiss broke up as he scrambled to catch it. David was immediately up from the table and chasing the piece of flying trash, and I sat back down, laughing at him. Our moment of intimacy had come and gone, ruined by a greasy fish box. He finally snagged it before it could fly into the river, and I started packing up our trash and stuffing it into the carryout sack. The picnic table was neat and tidy when we left it, but inside I was a confused mess.

Kissing David Standish—enjoying it—and wanting more. It was absurd. He was older, and we had little in common. On the ride back, neither of us mentioned the brief romantic interlude, and many thanks to Kenny G for stepping into the stone-silent breach and playing beautifully and louder on the way back to Meadowbrooke. When David walked me into the lockup and to my room, supporting me at the waist as a boyfriend would do, I mentally flogged myself to avoid sinking into that delicious physical comfort. His arm at my waist was nothing personal—just a mechanism to keep me from tipping over, which still remained a possibility. David was not my boyfriend—not a boy at all, which was part of my mental difficulty with our little accidental rendezvous. The fact that I considered him my friend weighed heavily on my mind after he left and I slowly got ready for bed. I didn't want to ruin a longstanding friendship by having some kind of drug-induced, emotional attachment that would disintegrate as soon as the prescriptions for my meds ended.

That had to be it. I was still on some medicine. Otherwise, I wouldn't have kissed David.

But that didn't explain why he had created my conundrum by unexpectedly kissing me.

Chapter Eight

On Christmas morning, Kim breezed into my room holding a long, thin package wrapped in shiny red paper.

My mood suddenly sank. "Oh no. Kim, you bought me a gift? I didn't get you anything." I stared at the parcel, frustrated with myself. "I'm sort of low on funds, honestly. Didn't buy any Christmas gifts this year."

She chuckled. "That's cool. I didn't get you anything either. This item was coming your way, and I was kindly allowed to present it to you. So I wrapped it." She set it carefully under my tiny Christmas tree, where it teetered precariously on the small table. We both watched it seesaw.

"I think I should open it so it doesn't fall while I'm at breakfast. Don't you?"

She looked as excited as a three year old about to rip the paper off her own gift. But she was excited about me opening mine—the kind of behavior I had learned to expect from Always Cheerful Kim. She rescued the package and presented it to me. I was standing with old Silver, about to make the trek to breakfast. I took a side step so I was leaning against the bed and wouldn't suddenly forget to remain vertical. And I ripped off the shiny paper in one second flat.

"Oh wow. Man, this is something." My eyes were suddenly full of tears, yet I started to laugh. I held it out in front of me and tapped the floor. "A cane. Looks like a sports model too." It also had a jingle bell hanging from the handle by a bit of ribbon.

She laughed and gave me a quick hug. "Nothing is too good for our Princess. You use it in good health, okay? Merry Christmas!" She stepped back to give me space. "So. You ready to give it a try?"

Leo was summoned and the two of them walked on either side of me all the way to the dining room. I was a little unsteady, but not bad, and could figuratively feel the wind rushing through my hair as I began to master this new level of physical dexterity. Once I was seated for breakfast, Leo and Kim excused themselves. As I realized these days, I was not the only person at Meadowbrooke, but I definitely was one of the luckiest ones there.

The staff made Christmas Day as festive as possible. Bright red and green napkins on the everyday white tablecloths, centerpieces of greenery, sparkle-dipped pine cones, and colorful plastic bells that almost looked metal. I sniffed at the greenery, but it had lost any fresh pine odor it might have had. I pushed away the regret that I hadn't been able to visit the Standish Christmas tree farm this year and inhale lung fulls of that wondrous scent.

I got loads of comments about graduating to the cane. Steven, the counselor, caught up to me after breakfast—not exactly a difficult task.

"Merry Christmas, Emily. I see you've got a new ride. Very nice." He fell into step beside me.

"Thanks, Steven. Pretty cool to be without the training wheels. I almost feel like a grown-up."

"I'd say you're doing great. Do you think you'll be leaving us soon?"

"It looks more like it every day." I stopped and faced him. "Look, Steven, I'm sure I've been a rotten patient for you, and I apologize."

He shrugged. "I'm here if you want to talk. I'm also here if you don't want to talk."

"I'm doing okay, thanks. I'm surprised you're working on Christmas."

"Holidays are hard for a lot of people. I'll be here all day."

"It takes a special person to do your job, Steven. You're really good at it."

"Thanks, Emily. I appreciate that." He looked down at the cane again. "Have you named old Silver's replacement?"

I followed his gaze and contemplated momentarily. "Hmm. I think he looks like a Lightning."

Steven laughed and shook his head. "You're one of a kind, Emily."

Suddenly, Matthew Singer popped into view, bundled in a blue snowsuit that made a swishing sound when he walked, and wearing a hand-knitted, red toboggan cap pulled down over his eyebrows. "Em'ly! Merry Christmas!"

Steven greeted Matthew and moved along.

Behind Matthew, his mother Melissa approached— holding hands with Jim Standish, David's brother. Well, this was interesting. All three of them were glowing with happiness. Wow, a lot can happen when you're out of circulation for a couple of months.

"Merry Christmas, Emily. Oh my. I see you've moved up to a cane." Melissa gave me a cautious hug, and we moved into a small seating area.

"Yep. It's been a great Christmas so far."

Matthew stood next to me, one hand on the chair's arm rest and the other on my knee. Looking up into my face, he asked, "Did Santa bring you sumpin', Em'ly?"

I showed him the cane. "See? It even has a jingle bell."

Matthew carefully nudged the bell so it would tinkle. He beamed up at me.

"A cane means I'm getting so much better I can use this instead of the big walker I had last time you saw me."

"Yay! You get better every day." He leaned close to me and whispered, "Mommy said I can't ask again are you coming to live with us."

"Okay," I whispered as I hugged him tightly. "Did Santa come to your house, Matthew?"

"Yes! He bringed me a track with cars and trucks. Even a police car."

"Cool. Santa always knows the right gift to bring, doesn't he?"

Matthew nodded solemnly. "'Cuz I write him a letter. And guess what. Miss Lillian maked me this hat." He tugged the red toboggan down a little lower. "It's a boggancap." Taking a couple of steps backward, he pulled gently at the nylon fabric encasing his little body. "Mr. Jim gave me this snowsuit. It's the same color of his truck." He stopped, looking at each of us in turn. "Blue," he said quietly.

We all laughed.

"Yes, I see it's blue. That's your favorite color, isn't it, Matthew?"

He nodded again. His face was red and sweaty with all that gear on. Obviously, he was thrilled with the cap and snowsuit. I silently wished Melissa good luck getting them off him at bedtime.

Jim cleared his throat. "Emily, I just had to ride along today and say hello. I've been hearing good reports but wanted to see you myself.

"Yep. Doing great. Thanks for the Christmas tree for my room. It's darling. Dad told me you and David gave us our trees this year. That was really nice."

He shrugged. "We were glad to. It was all we could think of at the time when Marcus came out to get the trees. That and a bag of goodies Mom threw together."

I patted my stomach. "I've had more of Lillian's famous cookies than is wise for someone with reduced activity level. Not that I wouldn't eat a box of them if they materialized right now. I have no willpower."

"You'll lose those few extra pounds once you get moving again, honey." Melissa patted my hand. "Any update on when you might be released?"

"No, but I think it's getting close. I imagine you'll hear me cheering all the way in Serendipity. Or maybe you'll hear the staff of Meadowbrooke cheering. I haven't been the easiest person to deal with."

"Really? That's surprising." Melissa really did look as if it were.

"Oh yeah. I'm sure anybody here could tell you stories about my terrible attitude. It's changed though. Being here has been good for me, and I'm the last person to have expected those words to come out of my mouth."

That's when my mom and dad, Ben, Hannah, Taylor, and Gran appeared. Jim, Matthew, and Melissa left so there was more seating, and by the time my first wave of family was preparing to leave, Uncle Jamison and Aunt Darlene and their kids swept into the room. That's the way it was all day. One group would finish visiting just as the next one arrived. I was wiped out by dinner time, when Lightning and I made our quiet way down the hall. I hadn't managed to return to my own room since breakfast and had had to dive into a public restroom between visits and plates of goodies. The sound of Christmas music and people talking and laughing receded as I closed the door to my room and sighed with relief. I turned on the lights for my tiny Christmas tree and sat in a chair near it. I was still there, dozing in my chair, when I heard a knock at the door.

"Emily? Okay if we come in, dear?" It was Lillian Standish's sweet voice.

"Oh." I sat upright and wiped my face with the back of one sleeve in case I had drooled in my sleep. "Sure, Lillian." The door started to open, and light spilled in from the hallway. "Just hit the light switch. I've been basking in the glow of a Standish Christmas tree."

She came in, followed by her daughter Carla—and David. "Emily dear, I hate to interrupt your Christmas light basking," Lillian said, leaning down to kiss my forehead. "We won't stay long. Just wanted to come in and wish you a Merry Christmas."

Carla and David gave me identical side-arm hugs. It wasn't a surprise from either of them, but from David, considering that evening by the river, it was a blow. I had started to let myself believe he was interested in me. I'd decided I was definitely interested in him.

Well, crap. Another relationship ends, and this one hadn't even begun.

But Lillian and Carla were apparently unaware of anything unusual between David and me, and if he wasn't interested after all, I needed to let go of that short-lived dream for the sake of our families' harmony.

I pictured childhood joint holidays with the Standish family and managed a sincere smile. "This is a long way to come to just say Merry Christmas. Thanks for making the effort, everybody."

David leaned against the wall and Lillian sat on the edge of the bed, her hand on the back of my chair. Carla stood a couple of feet away near the tree. "We wanted to see you, Emily," David said. "But we also had a secondary motive. Mom suggested we give Francie, Brad, and their son a little time to themselves. Brad and Joseph just arrived the day before Christmas Eve, and they haven't had Francie to themselves until now."

Carla chuckled. "I'm sure it's been a culture shock for Brad and Joseph to be at the tree farm at Christmas time. They'd never experienced it before, always coming nearer the first of the year. They were really good help in spite of being new to the work."

Lillian sighed. "Francie has made quite a sacrifice, staying with me all these months since Harry died. I appreciate it—we all do—but it has been a hardship for her own little family. It's so difficult to know how much to do for someone and when it's simply time to let them deal with situations in their own way."

Carla and David looked at Lillian quickly, but she was focused on my tiny tree.

Carla slid her jacket aside. "Emily, do you remember how our family and yours used to get together for holidays and birthdays?"

"Sure. We'd pour into Grandma Reba and Grandpa Geoffrey's house or Lillian and Harry's. You four kids, and me, and eventually Ben. He and I always thought it was great because you guys were older and so cool. I don't remember the twins ever being part of it."

"Hmm. No." Lillian shook her head, looking at us now. "By the time Hannah and Taylor were born, my four were nearly grown. They didn't have time for such things. Life sure changes when you're not looking."

It sure does.

"Now, for instance, with this new romance…."

Lillian hesitated, and I held my breath. So I hadn't been wrong about David's attraction to me?

"Not that it's a surprise to me, of course, but the timing and how it came about—well, it's a welcome bit of happiness in a world that has too much sadness. I've even begun to imagine what the wedding will look like."

She was getting way ahead of reality, talking about David and me that way. It had only been a couple of kisses, after all. What in the world had he said to her?

Carla sighed. "Jim and Melissa always did make a great couple."

Oh—that romance. The actual romance, not the one that's only in my head.

"Um, they came here today and brought Matthew. I hadn't realized they were seeing each other."

David nodded, looking just past my right ear. "Yep. Good to have them back together. It was a lot of wasted time in between."

Lillian tipped her head, considering his statement. "Who are we to say? Maybe the years they were apart were necessary for some reason." She nodded and jumped up, surprisingly agile for her age. "All right, children. Shall we head back home and let Emily get some rest?" Lillian kissed my forehead again and hugged me. "We'll see you back in Serendipity before long, dear."

I was relieved when Christmas Day ended. Having loads of company had been fun but exhausting. And it was totally my own fault the visit from Lillian, David, and Carla had been almost embarrassing. Thank goodness I hadn't looked at David with big puppy dog eyes at the wrong moment. I guess I was lucky to realize he definitely wasn't interested in me as anything but a kid sister. I could be happy for Melissa and Jim and little Matthew. I fell asleep remembering how cute he'd been, red-faced and happy in his snowsuit and toboggan.

I was awakened by the disembodied voice a few hours later.

Turn the page, Emily.

And I was all alone in my room with no one there to blame for the interruption or to ask about its meaning.

Chapter Nine

A couple of days later, Dr. Jay came to visit me. I was just about to go to the dining room for breakfast and was dressed in my usual attire—black yoga pants, long knit top, and my new lime green walking shoes. Leo had said I needed to get used to regular footwear again instead of living constantly in house shoes.

"Miss Emily. What a delight to see your very fine face this good morning."

"Hi, Dr. Jay. Nice to see you too. How are you doing?"

He looked at me thoughtfully. "I do not think you have ever asked me such a question in the past, Miss Emily." He smiled more broadly. "How indeed am I?"

"You're kidding. I've never asked how you are?"

He shrugged. "The concern has always been about you, my dear Emily Kincaid. Has it not?"

"I guess." It had been his concern as my doctor, but I also think he was saying my own concern had always been about me. Or was I reading too much into his statement?

He glanced down at a clipboard and back up to smile at me again. "There is some wonderful news, Miss Emily."

"I'm busting out of here?"

He laughed. "Indeed. Your family can take you home to complete your recuperation. There will be follow-up checks at my office, of course."

"Of course." Whatever got me on my way as quickly as possible.

He set the clipboard on the side table and held his hands out to me. I stood up without much help, and he peered deep into my eyes. "Miss Emily, we discussed once before the fact that your second chance in this life should be met with gratitude."

"Yes, I know. I am grateful. I—well, I've gotten to know this aide, Kim, and she's a really good influence."

"Ah yes. Our very dear Kimberly Rose. What an angel she is to so many."

"Did you know she gets to go to nursing school? She's thrilled."

He nodded. "I have heard this. It is very good news for her and for all the people she will touch in her work."

"She's been an inspiration to me, and she's only an aide." I chuckled.

Dr. Jay shook his head. "There is no *only*. She is a nurse aide who cares about doing the very best she can. Not every aide can go to school and become a nurse, but each can do her very best in the job she has. Such is true for each person on this earth. Not every American will be president, but each one should do his or her best at whatever job they have."

I sighed. "That's a lot of good advice. I don't have a job yet, but I'll keep that in mind."

"Ah, but you *do* have a job—living your life the very best way you can. That is your first and most important job. Do not let that fact escape your attention."

He released my hands and straightened to his full height which was considerable. "I will sign the paperwork for your release and look forward to hearing wonderful updates about your new life when you are at my office for follow-up." He retrieved the clipboard.

"Good-bye, Miss Emily. It has been my very great pleasure to observe your progress. Please give my kind regards to your family."

"Sure thing, Dr. Jay. Thanks so much!"

I immediately called my parents' house but when there was no answer, left a message, texted Danielle, Karly, and my brother Ben. I called Gran and had to leave a message there too. Frustrated, I went down for breakfast, my phone strapped to my side like Clint Eastwood might wear a six-shooter. The only difference was that Gran had made my phone holster, complete with some very sweet cross-stitch. Clint should be so lucky. I had the ringer turned down low so it wouldn't bother anyone, but I really hoped it would go off.

"Hey, Princess. I hear exciting news."

Finally, someone to share it with. I happily turned to meet Kim. "Yeah. So exciting my family isn't available to hear it. But I've left messages, sent some texts." I shrugged. "Decided I should go ahead and have my last fabulous breakfast here. I'll need my energy for all the work of moving out. Ha ha." I had maybe a duffel bag of clothes, a drawer full of get-well and thinking-of-you cards, a vase of daisies, and a slightly dry miniature Christmas tree. "I hope somebody brings me a coat to wear. Last time I went out, I could have used one."

But I hadn't needed it because David had let me wear his jacket. That seemed ages ago, and except for the visit with Lillian and Carla, I hadn't heard from him since. The vase of daisies in my room now had been brought to me by one of the other aides. "Left at the front counter" had been her explanation when she'd changed out the old ones for the new.

"If no one shows up to get you, I'll let you bunk with me." She laughed. "Of course, I live in a studio apartment on the third floor of a building with no elevator, and there's barely enough room for me and the cat. But you're welcome."

"Wow, you make it sound pretty enticing. I might have to take you up on that generous offer, Kim. Give me a few days to get up the stairs, okay?"

She chuckled and moved on with a waggle of her fingers, strolling down the hall to share her positive attitude with everyone in the vicinity. I remembered how Kim's smile had irritated me when she first entered my life. Now I wondered how much I'd miss seeing it on a nearly daily basis. In spite of our rocky start, Kim had become a mentor and friend.

My excitement at being released was immediately tempered by a sense of loss. But I wasn't allowed to dwell on it, because the word had gotten out about my leaving. Several people—nurses, aides, other patients— came over to me during breakfast, said kind words about me being pleasant to have around, which was a total surprise because I was pretty sure I'd been a pain a lot of the time. Everyone wished me well. There was even a doughnut with a candle stuck in it that someone brought me to help with the celebration. Although I didn't have a session scheduled, I went to the physical therapy area and said good-bye to Leo.

Mom arrived to pick me up, and there was a flurry of activity involved in moving my few belongings from my room to Mom's van. As I was buckling the seatbelt and she began chatting about stopping in for a quick visit to Gran and making my favorite dinner tonight, I looked with new appreciation at the low, nondescript building where I had spent so many weeks. Not only had Meadowbrooke and the people there given me the help I needed to physically function normally again, but they had also done a great deal for me mentally and emotionally. Not just Kim, Leo, and Steve, the counselor who had tried his best with me, but the whole staff and the patients too. Yep, it had been the place I needed. Now I had to figure out where I was going next.

Chapter Ten

The winter sun shone bravely through the sparkling clean windows of Gran's kitchen, but I knew the icy air outside would take my breath away and the wind cut like a knife. It was with a deep sense of contentment that I soaked up the atmosphere and love at this table where conversation always felt intimate. Today was an event since Mom, Gran, and I hadn't been in this spot together for months.

Gran poured her tea last and added two cubes of sugar and a dash of cream. "I'm glad Geoffrey and I put replacement windows in this house a few years ago. It makes all the difference toward keeping the place warm on a day like this." She stirred thoughtfully, looking out the back window where the bare branches of a large tree were waving in the wind. I doubt she was really seeing the tree. She sometimes got that faraway look when she talked about Grandpa.

My mom sipped her tea, carefully watching Gran's face. "Mother, have you given any more thought to what Marcus and I discussed with you the other day?"

Gran's gaze came reluctantly back indoors and settled on her daughter. "Marcus wants to know?"

"Well, both of us, really." Mom shifted in her chair, probably more uncomfortable with the topic than with the seating. "We just want what's best for you."

Gran looked at me and clasped my hand. "Emily, when they start saying that to you, it means they think you're incapable of making decisions for yourself."

Mom protested softly as I swallowed my response. I'd heard that a time or two myself. I guess they looked at Gran and me as kindred spirits.

"Jennifer, you and Marcus are sweet to be concerned, but I am absolutely fine." She winked at me. "Now, I'm dying to know what you've decided, Emily. What's next for you?"

Great. Shift the focus in my direction.

I took a deep breath. "I've thought about my future a lot lately. I need to make some changes." I looked at Mom too and hoped I appeared more confident than I felt. "My plan might seem a little drastic at first but nothing we can't deal with."

Mom blinked. I could see her steeling herself. She'd been through so much with me already.

"Meaning what?" Gran asked.

"Um. To start, I need to get rid of some things. Stuff I've accumulated over the years."

"That doesn't sound too bad," Mom said. You could almost see the sigh of relief waft from her lungs.

"I think it'll all work out great." I drank the last sip of my tea. Gran immediately refilled the cup and slid the sugar bowl and creamer toward me. "And I need to get my own place."

Mom nearly choked on her tea. "What? Now?"

"Yeah. I don't expect you and Dad to pay for it, so don't worry, okay? With Ben in college now and the twins starting in the fall, I realize the family finances are stretched."

Mom took a moment trying to form words but was in shock. "We'll see," she managed finally. "We can talk about some options if that's the direction you want to go." She reached to the teapot and refilled her cup, maybe wishing it was something stronger. It must be constant stress to be a parent. I felt sorry for her and regretted adding even more to her load, but she needed to know.

"This is not a whim, Mom. I know I can't do it immediately, but it needs to be soon. I'd think you and Dad would be ready to have me out from underfoot."

"Sweetie, you're not underfoot. Listen—we'll talk about it tonight at dinner, okay? I'm glad you have some ideas for your future. Honestly, I'm thrilled about that. Let's see what we can do."

Thank goodness neither of them asked me any details, because I hadn't exactly figured those out yet. But after the experiences of the last few months, my outlook on life had changed drastically. I had a sense of urgency that I need to be doing my life's work. As Dr. Jay had referred to it—"the job of living your life the very best way you can. That is your first and most important job."

Truth be told, I'd had a boatload of jobs in my life—factory, clerical, fast food, cleaning, babysitting—but I knew without a doubt that at no point in time had I lived my life the best I could. In fact, I had botched it quite thoroughly at times. All I had right now was intuition, or something equally impossible to pin down, telling me that once I got started in the right direction, events would begin to fall into place. Plus I had Kim's cell number in case I felt panicky.

Coming back to Serendipity was great but also a challenge. I had lived here my whole twenty-five years and so far had achieved next to nothing. People in a small town remember stuff about you—the time you hit a baseball out of the park and won the conference game, the first place finish in the state spelling bee, the incredible portrayal of the title character in *Annie*. Those memorable accomplishments were made respectively by my brother Ben, my friend Karly, and my sisters Hannah and Taylor, who shared the role of Annie back in their more malleable years. The only feat I was likely famous for in Serendipity was almost killing myself in a one-vehicle wreck. Although it was also possible I was famous for quitting a lot of jobs or surviving a lot of relationship failures. I had nowhere to go but up.

Mom pushed her chair back and stood. "Ready, Emily? I hate to break up the party, but I need to get home and start dinner."

Gran rose too.

"Okay." I got up and grabbed Lightning. Mom and I put on our coats and Gran, who was there to help, if needed, smiled happily to see I did fine. She pulled her coat on too, so she could walk to the van with us.

"Watch this." I was proud of my high marks in dealing with vehicle ingress and egress—I'd improved greatly since the evening David took me out in his car. I seamlessly made the maneuver into the front passenger seat and pulled the cane in to rest it by my leg. Gran high-fived me. Mom hugged Grandma Reba and kissed her cheek, and Gran leaned down and kissed mine before stepping back and gently closing the car door.

I relaxed back against the head rest and took a deep, self-satisfied sigh. My first day out of Meadowbrooke—the first day of the rest of my life and a chance to be okay with being myself, by myself. I was determined to make it.

I felt strong mentally and even physically. The past was behind me. I would never again be interested in a relationship such as the one I had with Adam. It had been broken from the beginning because we were both too much in love with ourselves to love the other one.

Chapter Eleven

True to her word, Mom fixed some of my favorites for dinner that night. She had also baked bread that morning, so a basket was filled with thick slices of homemade bread and next to it, jars containing some of the summer's jam production—blackberry or strawberry. One huge perk of having a mom who didn't have a job away from the house was the constant awesome food. After a few minutes of digging into the meal with appreciation, I took a break to bring up the topic Mom and I had discussed earlier at Gran's house.

"Um. You know I appreciate you all moving me back here since—well, since I don't have another home right now. I'm sure it's been a hardship on the whole family for me to be in the hospital and rehab." I was afraid to learn the cost of my medical bills—air ambulance, hospital, rehab facility. Somehow I would pay them back for all of it. "And you're really nice to let me come back here…but I think it's important for all of us to get our lives back to some kind of normal. So as soon as possible, I really need to get my own place."

There was about one second of dead silence.

"I want her room!" both twins yelled.

"Girls." Mom gave them the look, and both Taylor and Hannah shut up.

Mom shot a look to Dad and then to me. "Sweetie, we can help you get up the stairs to your room until you're comfortable maneuvering on your own."

Dad nodded. Poor guy was likely sitting there wishing he'd had three boys and a girl instead of the other way round. With Ben away at college, Dad was really in the minority.

"Mom, Dad, I appreciate that. I know you're willing to help me. You've done so much already." I clasped my hands together under the table to keep them from shaking. "Really, I need to be on my own as soon as possible. I love and appreciate you, but this is so important. It's fine with me if my stuff is moved out of my room upstairs—into the old summer kitchen, maybe. I just need a place to sleep and to not be a burden."

Mom looked at me, likely detecting my voice breaking with emotion. She put her hand on my shoulder and made me look directly into her eyes. "Emily. You are not a burden."

"Mom," I whispered. "I have to get out of here. I have things to do." I didn't have particulars to share but felt a sense of immediacy.

Taylor rolled her vivid blue eyes and tucked a strand of perfectly straight, strawberry blond hair behind one ear. "Things to do? You can barely walk."

Mom took a little out of the bowl of mashed potatoes and pushed it toward Taylor with a look. I could see she was playing the role of peacemaker again. It always bothered her more than the rest of us when we didn't get along. "Emily, the old summer kitchen is so small."

I gulped some water. "There's room for a bed, a dresser, and some clothes. And the bathroom is right next door. It would be very temporary." I shifted my focus to my father. "Dad? Is it a lot of extra work for you to move my stuff down?"

Mom looked at him, and I detected a glimmer of hope in her eyes. If I convinced Dad to clear out that room, she'd be thrilled because she had asked him dozens of times.

He slowly cut a piece of steak, speared it with his fork, and lifted it to his mouth.

Stalling.

I had lived with Adam for a couple of years, and prior to that, Karly and Danielle and I had shared an apartment. But my room in my parents' home had always been kept for me, just in case I came back, which to my embarrassment, I always had. It was full of school memorabilia, stuffed animals, books, and tons of clothes none of us would ever wear again. It was just generally *full*.

Dad swallowed, set down his cutlery, and met my gaze.

"Emily, you and I can look at the room after dinner. I imagine it's smaller than you remember. Your room upstairs is at least three times the square footage."

"Thanks for considering it, Dad. I'd rather have something small. Really. And it's just until I can get my own place."

Taylor and Hannah looked hopeful, and Mom's soft intake of breath meant she thought it might happen too. They all had their reasons for wanting me to get that little room, but my reason was vastly different. The summer kitchen, located at the back of the house, was literally and figuratively on the way out of my parents' house. At long last—but this time, forever.

After dinner, Dad and Lightning and I went to the

summer kitchen. Dad opened the door, flipped on the light and went into the room first, picking a small tool box up off the floor and setting it near the wall.

Wow. It looked worse than I remembered.

"Emily, Your mother has suggested I'm a hoarder, but that's not the case. Everything in this room is useful."

I looked up at him, my ruggedly handsome father who women of all ages swooned for. Yeah, he was also a slob.

"Okay, Dad. So it's all got to stay here, and I can't have the room?" Just as well get to the heart of the matter.

"Well...no." He spoke slowly, looking around. "Most everything could go into my workshop in the garage. It's handy to have tools right here when I need to do something in the house, you see." He arched a brow, inviting me to agree.

"It would be so cool, Dad, if I could have this little space. I can't stand the idea of you and Mom having to help me up and down the stairs for every meal or when I need to go to appointments." I picked my way carefully around the miscellany, eventually reaching one of the windows and peering through. "Isn't it funny I've almost never seen the view from this window?"

My room upstairs was on the other side of the house and looked out at the neighbor's window to the east. This room, in spite of its small size, had two tall windows with views of the road that ran along the side of the house, and the field across the road. The unencumbered panorama of what was now a stubble field of dried corn stalks and a pale blue sky seemed exotic in comparison to wondering when the neighbor would get the peeling paint scraped and recoated on his big house.

I continued my campaign. "It's so close to the bathroom too, and the girls and I wouldn't have to share. As slow as I am, I can imagine how that's going to be."

He sighed, likely imagining fights over bathroom time. The little one adjacent to this was mostly just used as a powder room if we had guests for dinner. All the bedrooms were upstairs. My parents had a bathroom to themselves, and we four kids had grown up sharing or running downstairs when absolutely necessary. We'd always been better at yelling at each other through the closed bathroom door on the second floor than opting for coming down here. It would be awkward to get in and out of a tub on my own now, and I was slow even at showering. Our shared bathroom upstairs had a shower in the tub, but this little one downstairs was just a sink, toilet, and shower stall. I could manage here by myself. Showering 101 had been one of my classes, so to speak, at Meadowbrooke.

Dad looked overwhelmed. "I suppose it's the best option."

"Wonderful!" Mom was standing in the doorway, looking as pleased as a lottery winner.

Dad's response was more of a grimace. "It'll be a bit of work, but we'll manage well enough."

Mom stepped cautiously into the room. "Perhaps, eventually, my mother will want to move in here."

Dad shook his head. "I don't see you talking her into that, Jen."

I couldn't imagine Gran ever wanting this tiny room, or to live with our family at all. But you never know. I was just starting to come to terms with my own changes and wondered how my family and friends would handle them once they became more apparent.

Dad picked up the tool box he had moved when we first entered the room, and in the other hand a paint can. Mom unlocked and opened the door in the south wall that led outside, and he strode out and down the single step toward the two-car garage which also housed his workshop. There went load number one. I knew it was hard for Dad to give in on this, and I promised myself that as soon as I was physically able, I'd help him organize his workshop if he wanted me to.

A few minutes later, Mom rousted Hannah and Taylor, who helped Dad carry stuff out of the old summer kitchen for the rest of the evening. Mom drove to the grocery and got some boxes so Dad could pack up the hodgepodge that was in the built-in cabinets. An amazing amount of stuff had been in that room. I didn't have the heart to watch, and Dad shooed me away from trying to help pack the cardboard cartons. He wanted to organize as he went, he said.

That was a Monday. I slept in my own bed upstairs and stayed there except for dinner because it was a scary event getting up and down the stairs. We had to have Dad help to ensure Mom and I didn't tumble down the steps together. Each evening after work and dinner, Dad spent time clearing out the room. I piddled around, trying to help, or at least not slow progress.

"Room's cleared out. You'll want to paint." Dad muttered to Mom as he sat down for dinner Wednesday night.

Mom, Taylor, and Hannah looked at me.

"I don't need it painted. It's just temporary."

We all trooped into the empty room after dinner. The walls were a dingy yellow, scraped in lots of places and generally ugly.

Mom sighed. "Pick a color, Emily."

I shrugged. "I'd like white. But I didn't want this to be so much work."

Hannah rolled her eyes. "Gag. White? Seriously."

"White? Not something pretty?" asked Taylor, mirroring her twin's reaction.

"White will be pretty." I began to visualize the completed room. "Not off-white either. Bright white, the color of marshmallow crème or clouds."

"It will certainly look...clean." Mom tried to shrug off a frown.

The great aspect about the painting is that I couldn't do much, meaning the twins had to help and they had to do a good job or do it all over again. Mom has always been picky about home improvement projects. Dad can build about anything and Mom can decorate it. She loves rich color, and these would be the only white walls in our entire house.

"Emily, I hope you appreciate all our hard work." Taylor and Hannah said that to me a few times while they worked on the little room. Not only had they painted, but they'd had to scrape old, chipped paint first and smooth it with sand paper.

"Of course I appreciate it, girls. Just as much as you appreciate getting my big room upstairs." They both brightened at that. They didn't even seem to care who got my room and who had to stay in the smaller room they now shared. The point for them was having their own space. The point for me in the move was similar but also vastly different.

It was January, and our area had more snow and way more cold and wind than usual. It was the best time of year to be stuck inside with a leg that didn't want to function well. A couple of snow days from school meant the girls got my room finished and started working on their own. The upstairs hallway and Ben's vacant room were piled with my furniture and stuff.

I was adamant that I didn't want to move the conglomeration into my new space.

Mom chuckled. "Emily, sweetie, of course you want your things!"

I didn't want them, and the idea of being surrounded by all that stuff made me feel claustrophobic. Maybe it was because I had spent so much time where the furniture was sparse and utilitarian, and my belongings were limited to the few items of clothing I actually wore and a vase of flowers. Seriously, what else did a person need, I wondered, but there was no reason to start a confrontation about it. Somehow I needed to shed extraneous items in order to move on with my life. I knew that in my heart but hadn't come up with a good way to make it happen.

I shrugged and stood in the living room at the bottom of the stairs. Looking up, if I leaned a certain way, I could see some of my clutter stacked in the upstairs hall. How had I collected so much when, in my entire life, I hadn't been anywhere or done anything? Pretty ridiculous, and this didn't include the boxes Adam had packed up which were now in my parents' garage.

The sun shone brilliantly outside, making the living room brighter than usual. I walked over to look out on the snow-covered lawn beyond the picture window. It was gorgeous. Mom came over and stood at the window with me, her arm around my shoulders.

"Mom, I know I'm lucky to enjoy winter from in here, safe and warm. Can you see that I can't stay long-term? You and Dad are awesome and, most of the time, I don't even mind the twins that much. But...do you know what I mean when I say I have to start my life?"

"I think to some extent I do, Emily. We'll do what we can to help."

I nodded silently, pulled toward a future I couldn't see. All I knew was that in order to get there, I needed to pack light. The snowscape outside was enchanting, brilliant white, and pristine like the small room at the back of my parents' house. I stared out the window, wondering how to achieve such perfection with my life.

Chapter Twelve

Mom sighed. "We'll get your things carried downstairs as soon as possible. Your bed first, so you can sleep down here tonight."

She looked tired, and I figured we all were after days of working on the project. Dad would be hit up to help after dinner, as usual, of course. I knew he was more tired of it than the rest of us because he'd never wanted to start. Everyone was gaining something from this except Dad, who was losing real estate he'd claimed for his stuff. My brother Ben probably wasn't gaining or losing, since he seldom came home from college for even a weekend. I assumed we'd see very little of him from now on.

Taylor and Hannah ran down the stairs on the way to the kitchen.

"Girls, don't ruin your dinner. Your father is

bringing David Standish home to eat with us." Mom plumped the cushions on the sofas and stood in the center of the room to see what else might need attention before a guest arrived.

A little thrill ran through me. "Really? That's a surprise."

"I thought so too. But it works out. I was thawing a pan of lasagna for dinner and have Italian bread rising. David is evidently home for the weekend, and when he asked your father about you, I guess it seemed logical to invite him here to see how our patient is doing."

"Ugh. Weird." Hannah rolled her eyes and they went on through to the kitchen.

"Mom, I wish you wouldn't call me a patient."

"Sorry. It's just a word."

I lowered myself onto the piano bench, the only seating surface that wasn't likely to be plumped. "I know, but it makes me feel…pathetic."

"You're certainly not pathetic, Emily. You're very strong to be alive and doing so well in spite of the odds. Some people in town are calling it a miracle."

"I didn't—don't deserve a miracle."

Mom stopped fussing over the room and joined me

on the piano bench. "I'm not sure one gets to choose whether or not to get a miracle."

"It makes me uncomfortable to know people are saying that." I took a deep breath, knowing the people of Serendipity would say whatever they wished about whatever they chose.

The girls reappeared, each carrying a diet soda and bag of chips. "Why is David Standish coming here for dinner?" asked Taylor. "He's never done that before."

Mom shrugged. "Your father called and said he'd seen David in town and invited him. Everyone in Serendipity is concerned about Emily's progress. I've been telling people she's not strong enough to have much company. This will be a start."

"Oh, good. We get to have the whole town to dinner, one by one? As if our lives weren't already twisted because Emily...had that wreck." Hannah hastily amended whatever she'd been about to say, and the girls took the steps quickly.

Mom shook her head watching them. She took my hand in hers. "Do you remember the Standish family gave us our Christmas tree for free this past year and another for your room at Meadowbrooke? It was such a nice gesture." Her voice cracked with emotion. "That's just one example of how much love was shown to us by the people of Serendipity after you got hurt."

I noticed the clock and panic gripped me. "Mom, I've gotten out of my routine since coming home, but if we're going to have company, I'd better be sure not to run him off with my body odor. If I could have a change of clothes and some shampoo down here, I'll take a shower. That okay?"

She grinned and stood. "Sure it is, sweetie. I'll have the twins bring them down for you."

I didn't know who would be gladdest once I was able to manage on my own.

Slow as I was, and since Taylor and Hannah hadn't been in a hurry bringing things downstairs for me, when I heard the back door, I had just finished dressing, straightening my hair, and putting on makeup for the first time since the wreck. I looked in the mirror and decided I didn't look bad, considering. Brown hair parted on the side with super long bangs, brown eyes made up with the retro cat-eye look that was so popular. Sure, my skin was pale and I looked tired in spite of make-up, but still.

I tilted my head and held a mirror to the side. The scar along my jawline was going to be a reminder forever, I guessed, and I still couldn't get my swollen knee into jeans and was stuck with yoga pants. The girls had brought me a clean black pair, plus underwear, heavy socks, and a black V-neck shirt that made me look even more anemic.

143

To balance my Morticia look, the house smelled divine—Mom's lasagna is legendary in Serendipity—and her homemade bread is another of my favorites. My stomach began to growl, and I wished for a piece of candy or something to shut it up.

Maybe you think I was trying to impress David Standish or that I thought we were going to pick up where we left off by the Ohio River that night. But I knew that wouldn't happen. David was just a friend of the family. He was ten years older than I, and cosmopolitan because of his work, where I was just plain Serendipity-boring. He'd watched me grow up, a snot-nose elementary school kid when he was a cool, popular upperclassman at SHS. He was available now as far as I knew, but with David, his status varied from week to week.

David Standish was just a handsome, older guy who lived a few miles from us on the weekends and during the Christmas tree season. Sure, back in the day I might have had a little bit of a crush on him, but that was ancient history. And except for Lillian and Gran, our families' closeness was history too, in all but surface pleasantries.

I heard Dad and David come in and walk down the hall toward the kitchen because the back door by the driveway is near the little bathroom where I was fussing over myself. It made me fuss faster, and at last I decided I had to go with what I had. I wadded up my dirty clothes and used a mop handle to poke them into a corner of the broom closet as I went by since I didn't have a hamper downstairs yet. I yearned to greet David without my cane but decided I wasn't quite ready for that.

David and Dad were leaning on one of the kitchen counters while Mom pulled lasagna out of the oven. David was holding a bottle of wine.

"Help you with that, Jennifer?" David asked.

She looked at him, then at Dad, who winced slightly, realizing he should have offered. Her face was a little red from being near the stove. "That's okay, David. I've got it. Marcus will show you where the wine screw is. Thanks again for bringing that." She carried the steaming lasagna into the dining room and set it on the awaiting trivets.

"Need me to do anything, Mom?" She looked at me as I neared the kitchen and did a double-take because of the makeup. Maybe I'd gone overboard.

"Emily. Well. I think we're okay. The girls set the table."

David opened the wine bottle with a flourish but immediately set it, the opener, and cork on the bar and came over to me. "Emily, you look great. Will you break if I hug you?"

My heart might, but not my bones. "Go ahead and let's find out," I said softly.

David put his arms around me oh-so-gently. He was tall and strong and smelled delicious as usual. I sighed happily, remembering the kiss we had shared at the picnic table.

He let go too soon but as gently as he'd started. That was good, because if he'd released me quickly, I might have done a header right there.

"Wow, Emily, you look better each time I see you."

"Good to know. Last time you saw me ambling around, I was still on old Silver, but as you see I've graduated to Lightning here." I tapped my cane on the floor in introduction.

"Nice ride. Much more sleek. And I'm sorry I didn't get back to see you after—" He faltered. "—after Christmas."

Nor a visit by yourself after the kiss. "It's okay." But it wasn't. In spite of telling myself not to want it, I kept hoping we could become more than friends.

He rubbed the back of his neck. "Work has been more demanding lately. I had the month off to help with

Christmas tree season as usual, but after that, all hell seemed to break loose." He stopped and shook his head. "Sorry about that. I didn't come here to talk about work."

"I think this is everything," Mom interrupted brightly, carrying baskets of homemade Italian bread from the kitchen to the dining room. Dad followed with a big bowl of home-canned, green beans from last summer's garden, and an enormous tossed salad.

David picked up the wine bottle, and Dad snagged four glasses from the china cabinet.

Mom went to the base of the staircase and called the twins, and in a minute they dragged their way down to join us. They looked particularly out of sorts. Must be some kind of social media drama going on.

"Hannah, Taylor, say hello to our guest," Dad prodded them. They muttered something unintelligible in David's general direction.

I made my way to the big oak dining table. Mom had put a couple of leaves in the table, so there was plenty of space. The seating order was Dad, Mom, David, me, Hannah, Taylor.

"Hey. No wine glasses for us?" Taylor asked.

"Not for a few years yet," Dad said.

"It's not like anybody would know if we had a little drink." Hannah muttered as she grabbed a thick slice of bread and passed the basket to Taylor. That was it. No incessant complaining about the wine, as they would have done without company right here.

I picked up my wine glass and tried to remember what to do. Swirl it around a little, I thought, and sniff the aroma. Smelled okay, but when I took a sip, it tasted, unfortunately, like wine.

"You're not a fan of dry wine, Emily?" David took a sip of his and set it down.

No, not a fan, and not even a tiny bit cultured. Another way in which David and I were opposites.

Conversation was a little awkward at first. Food was passed, and we dug in. What a treat to have Mom's lasagna—it tasted even better than I remembered.

David chewed appreciatively, even closing his eyes for a second. "Jennifer, I think this is the best lasagna I've ever eaten. I know it's a specialty of yours, but I think you've somehow improved on perfection."

"Thank you," Mom said, looking proud.

Dad grinned. "You can see it's a struggle not to overeat around here."

"Illness? Death? Call Jennifer's lasagna line."

Taylor laughed at her own inappropriate joke, as did Hannah.

Dad frowned at them but spoke to David. "It's true to an extent. She makes them often when there's a need for food to be carried in to a family." He turned to Mom. "Jen, how many do you have in the freezer?"

"Two or three. I like to be ready if someone calls but not keep them frozen too long."

I took another bite. "Lucky us it was time to rotate one out. Thanks, Mom."

"You're welcome, sweetie."

"Seems I remember one of these appearing at my parents' house after Dad's funeral." David looked from face to face around the table. "I sure appreciate the dinner invitation. Everybody has been so concerned about Emily and all of you. I miss a lot of what's said in town since I'm gone so much."

"That could be partly good," Mom said. "There's usually a hefty amount of gossip going around. You're better off without that, I'd say."

David nodded. "Sure. I can do without the gossip. But I also don't necessarily hear good news." He looked at me. "Knowing how well Emily is doing, for instance." He winked at me and my stomach did a flip-flop entirely unrelated to the dinner.

"David, your mother and mine are coming over tomorrow morning. Emily is moving into a different room, and they wanted to come over and take a peek."

"Is that right?" David looked at me again. "Making changes, are you?"

"She sure is," Dad said, looking abused. "It's about got the best of me."

I took a deep breath. "It has been a big job for Dad, and I'm sorry about that. The move to the little room is just something I needed to do. Makes sense for everybody if I'm downstairs. Plus the twins get to spread out instead of having to share a room."

"Yeah, finally." Hannah and Taylor finished eating and excused themselves.

After dinner, Dad and David and I helped clear the table, despite the fact I was too slow to accomplish much.

"Why don't you just relax, Emily?" David asked, carrying more in one trip than I could in three.

"I need to work. I have to push myself, so I'll get stronger as quickly as possible. I don't always want to be dependent on my parents."

"That's a good attitude. I imagine you'll do great if you keep that up. You have so far."

The four of us sat in the living room for a little while. David talked about the tree farm, but not his "real" job. He caught us up on his family too. We had all been so focused on my situation for too long.

"Mom's doing really well. It's been almost a year since Dad died. Her strength got all of us through the Christmas season."

I shifted on the couch trying to get comfortable and not put my knee in a bind. "I imagine that was terribly hard, considering how much Harry loved the Christmas tree farm."

"Yeah. Somebody said he was just a few pounds and a white beard away from being Santa Claus himself. Because the tree farm was so important to him and Mom, we felt we needed to try to continue it. Went better than any of us expected." He sighed and his eyes got a faraway look as if he'd forgotten we were there. "It was amazing," he whispered.

"David?" I prompted after a long pause.

He started, but smiled at me. "Sorry. Anyway, when spring comes, we're going to put little weekend cabins around on the farm. It was Melissa's idea— Melissa Singer."

Dad leaned forward in his chair. "Really? That's interesting."

"Melissa's sure we'll get decent income from it. I hope she's right, because the more we make from those, the more easily we can pay people to do some of the work on the tree farm. Since I'm only home on weekends, and Francie was with Mom, and Carla was running her business, Jim did a lot of it on his own last year, on top of his law practice. It was hard on him. Of course, don't let him know I seem too sympathetic. Gotta keep the macho brother thing going."

He slapped his thighs and got up. "I should get out of here. I'm pretty bushed anyway. Long week, in a series of long weeks." We all stood up too. Everybody was quicker at it than I, since the sofa was deep and squishy. David held his hand gently at my waist until I was steady.

"Thanks for that." I looked up into his clear green eyes, nearly the shade of emeralds.

"You're welcome." His voice was so soft, and his eyes held mine captive. I could barely breathe. I really didn't want to go back to being just friends. Did he?

"Um…Want to see my new room?"

Delaying tactic.

"Absolutely. Lead the way." I did, which meant we all walked slowly. As we went, Dad told David about all his tools and supplies he'd taken out of the room and put into his workshop so the renovation could begin.

"I feel for you, Marcus. Being a bachelor, I don't worry much about how my house looks as long as I can find what I need when I need it. Place is getting pretty thick with dust these days too."

I cringed at the picture but was glad he hadn't gotten somebody else to clean for him. "You *still* haven't replaced me?"

"Now, Emily, who could possibly replace you?" he asked from just behind me.

"Oh, I don't know. A mannequin. A snail." I reached the doorway and stepped into the old summer kitchen and paused to flip the light switch. The space lit up, and I was overcome with pleasure at its unique simplicity.

"Wow. This is—really small."

"Yep. Just what I need."

He stepped into the middle of the room. "What will you actually have room for? A bed and a dresser?"

I leaned against a built-in bookcase. "Just about. Pretty cool, huh?"

"Oka-ay. I don't get it. I mean, I realize you can't do stairs right now." He looked from the room to me quickly. "You are getting better, right? I mean, you will eventually be able to maneuver on stairs?" He frowned in concern, and his gaze shifted to Mom and Dad.

"Yes. Yes, as far as we know," Mom said tiredly. I was glad I was going to make her life a little easier by eliminating the stairs. That surely was a positive.

"It's better if I'm down here. Easier for everybody."

"Except for moving all the stuff," Dad said with a sigh. "Twice."

"Don't worry, Dad. You won't have to move it again."

Dad crossed his arms. "There's no way it will all fit in here."

"A lot can be left in boxes just outside in the hallway. I'll go through them and decide what to keep."

"Emily is downsizing," Mom said, shaking her head.

David laughed. "You're a little young for that, aren't you?"

I grinned back at him but didn't respond. He wouldn't understand. It seemed nobody could understand, but that didn't change how I felt.

"I'll be glad to help you, Marcus. What's the timeframe? Do you have things to move down here now?"

Without intending to, I mentally compared David's unselfish effort this evening to Adam's spineless decision to toss my stuff into boxes and dump it all in my parents' driveway without speaking a word to any of us.

That's how it happened that everything I owned in the world, except, of course, my broken car, was stacked in the back hallway that night. In spite of his age, David seemed to be in decent shape. He didn't huff and puff from all the trips he and Dad made up the stairs to the hall by my old room. They also made trips back and forth from a corner of the garage where Dad had put the boxes Adam had dropped off. My life history was stacked neatly along the wall in the back hallway of my parents' house, and the antique dresser that had been upstairs my whole life was looking pretty against the white bead board in my new room.

There was something intimate about David helping set up my little twin-size bed, even though Dad was working with him. Mom laid a set of clean sheets, pillow, and pillow case on the foot of the bed. "I put your comforter in the wash, Emily. I don't know…the white comforter and all this white paint…."

"Perfect," I breathed.

"Thank you for your help, David. I think I owe you another dinner," Mom said while he stretched his back.

"I'll take you up on that, Jennifer. You all just say the word, and I'm here."

"I promise not to make you carry twenty-five years of accumulation next time," I said.

He winked. "You didn't make me do it this time, Emily. I volunteered, remember?"

"Yes." I told myself to calm down and not get all gaga over David Standish. Kiss or not, and in spite of winks and daisies, he was still just that older guy whose house I happened to clean.

Mom appeared with his coat and David pulled it on. He turned to me again. "You give me a call when you're ready to come back to work, okay? I'm holding the job for you."

"I sure will."

A minute later he was out the door, his presence replaced by a blast of frozen air.

"That was nice," Mom said, heading to the laundry room to check on my comforter.

I sagged against the door frame, ridiculously missing David. *Wow.* I needed to get out among people more if one evening with a non-family member had such a strong effect.

"I'll say it was nice." Dad kissed my forehead. "The first night in your little cell, Emily. I hope you'll like it as much as you think you will."

"Cell?"

"You know, like the monks have in monasteries. I gather it's a tiny room with just a bed and nightstand, a place to hang your clothes. So you don't have any focus but meditation, I guess."

"Oh. That sounds good."

"Guess I should have said nuns instead of monks." He ran a hand over his face. "I'm done in. Do you need anything else tonight?"

I shook my head, watching his expression. "Nope. I'm good."

"All right. I'll check with your mom and head upstairs." He went toward the laundry room, and I started the laborious process of making my bed. It took ten times as long as it would have before the wreck but, eventually, I had dealt with the sheets and pillow cases. Exhausted, I lowered myself onto it and saw Mom leaning on the doorframe.

She tiredly pushed away from the frame. "Oh,

Emily. I wanted to help you but knew you should do it yourself." She came in, hugging my comforter. I could feel the warmth radiating from it, and the light floral smell that said 'home' was a delight. In an instant, it was on my bed, and she stepped back and looked around the room. "I don't know, sweetie. It's a little plain. When Lillian and Grandma Reba get here, we'll get their ideas too. That should be fun, right?"

"I guess. Just don't get your hopes up, Mom. I want to keep it simple."

Chapter Thirteen

Saturday was just as cold and windy as Friday had been. The sky was a pale gray, and I wished for spring to arrive in Serendipity. Lillian Standish and my grandmother showed up mid-morning.

They stood just inside the doorway to my room and sighed. "Oh my," Grandma Reba said, hands clasped together. "It's so peaceful, isn't it?"

"Mmm." Lillian sighed. "Somehow it reminds me of Henry David Thoreau's little house on Walden Pond. Where's your plain wood desk and chair, so you can write a new version of *Walden*?" She put her arm around me gently. "I adore the room, Emily. It's lovely."

"What about all your things in those boxes in the hall?" Gran asked, sitting down on the bed. "Not to rain on your parade, but those must be dealt with—and sooner rather than later. Your mother won't be able to stand them out there for long. Believe me, she's my daughter, and I know her OCD ways."

Mom walked in. "Is that right?"

"Said with love, Jennifer, dear. Said with love." Gran grinned at her, and Mom pulled an exasperated face but couldn't help the smile that followed it.

Lillian stood in the center of the space, concentrating. "You know...I have a tiny, upholstered loveseat in my attic that might be ideal in here, Emily. You can borrow it for as long as you like, if it appeals to you. It would give you seating for a couple of guests."

"Thank you, Lillian. I appreciate the offer. I'll try to get over and look at it soon." That meant someone had to drive me, of course. How I hated being a constant burden.

Mom served delicious sandwiches on homemade bread and cream of tomato soup for lunch. The ladies were headed to a meeting in a little while and were pulling on their coats when I hurried in my current slow, methodical way toward my room. I moved a box to the side and opened the one at the bottom of that stack, scanning the contents.

"Lillian, do you have a computer?"

"No, I've resisted. My children think me very old-fashioned."

"If you're interested, I'd like for you to have this one. It's not new or fancy or particularly fast, but you can get online. Shop, find people on Facebook if you've lost track of someone and want to reconnect. Recipes, news, whatever you want."

She walked over and looked dubiously at the contents of the box. "I'll admit that since Harry died, I've considered it. He distrusted computers and anything related to them. But I wouldn't know where to begin."

"I can teach you some basics. You'll need Internet."

"But Emily, won't you miss your computer?" Lillian asked.

"I have a smart phone and can do everything on it that I used the desktop computer for. It would make me happy if you have it and enjoy it." I motioned around the room at the lack of extra space. "Plus, if you take it, I don't have to figure out how to squeeze it in here." A laptop would be nice to have someday, but I didn't have the money for one.

I was amazed that Lillian was interested. She was already paying for cable because Harry had watched a lot of sports, and she simply hadn't made any changes. She pulled out her cell and called the cable company, subtracted some TV channels, and added Internet. In my mind, Lillian's coolness rating continued to ratchet upward.

She ended the call. "Well, that's taken care of—at least for now. I'll see whether I like having a computer. I might be bringing it back to you." But she looked excited, which surprised and pleased me.

Mom carried the two boxes to Lillian's car. Lillian said Jim or David could carry it into her house, since the CPU was rather heavy. After the ladies had driven away, Mom was back in the hallway with me while I looked through another box.

"Emily, that was kind of you. I hope you won't regret giving the computer away."

"I won't," I said without a doubt. "I feel—I don't know, somehow *lighter*—just having it gone and knowing Lillian was the right person to get it."

Mom looked confused. "The right person to get it? Why do you say that?"

"Oh—I don't know." I wasn't sure why, but I felt it strongly. "I'll go help Lillian when she's ready. Gran said she would drive me, and while I'm there, I can look at that little loveseat Lillian said she'd loan me.

Hey, it'll get me out of the house for a while." Surely Mom needed a break from my constant presence. "But no painting my room orange while I'm out, okay?"

She laughed. "Deal. You know I wouldn't do that."

"I know you wouldn't, but I also know you'd love to brighten it up. Remember, my being here is only temporary, and so is the boring white."

Mom shook her head, and walked toward the kitchen, and I was alone to slowly pick through another box of stuff.

***

"Hey," Karly said when she and Danielle came for a visit one evening. "What's with all the boxes still in the hallway? You need some help sorting what to keep and what to store?"

"Thanks, but I'm the one who has to decide. Because it's not what to keep and what to store. It's either keep or get rid of." I looked up at her from a low stool in the hallway which made it easier to go through the boxes without them being dragged into my tiny room. "You know what, Karly? This is for you." I pulled a favorite, purple handbag out of the box and held it out to her.

"No. Seriously?" She hugged it to herself. "I've always loved this bag."

"Well, it's yours now. Enjoy. You might check to be sure there's nothing in it."

Still beaming, she set the bag on another box and carefully examined the interior. "Gum wrappers, nine cents," she mumbled, "and a pair of sunglasses." She put them on.

"Those look great on you," said Danielle. "I don't remember you wearing them, Emily. Are they new?"

I tipped my head, noticing how perfect the glasses were on Karly. "Not new, but not me. Enjoy, Karly."

"Awesome! It's great timing, because I sort of sat on my sunglasses recently, and I hadn't found any I like." She pushed the glasses up onto her head and dropped the case back into the purple handbag.

"Excellent. My second satisfied customer," I said.

"Who was the first one?" Karly asked.

"Lillian Standish. I gave her my computer. Still need to get it set up and show her how to use it for some basic operations, but I think it's going to work out great. Since Harry died and her daughter Francie went back to Florida, she's alone in that big house quite a bit. A little social media time might be fun for her."

Danielle laughed. "So are you going to give everything away?"

I shrugged. "No real plan. I'll do what feels right. See how well it worked out for Karly? Don't make fun, Danielle. There might be something in one of these boxes that's just what you need."

Danielle leaned over the one I was working in. "Hmm. I don't see an eligible millionaire in there.

I gestured toward the line of cartons. "Don't give up, hope, girl. There are plenty of uncovered treasures."

"Yeah, right. Hey! Do you know what you should do? Why not make up some cute paper shopping bags with a logo, and your satisfied customers like Lillian and Karly—and hopefully me—can carry them to advertise you're offloading some good stuff. You might have people coming to your door and buying it. It could bring in some spending money, even when you can't really get out and have a job."

My breath caught. "Oh, Danielle, what a terrific idea. It's the wrong time of year for a yard sale without a chance of frostbite, but to open a little shop would be such fun."

Danielle nodded, and her eyes were bright with the excitement of our snowballing idea. "Cool. And—what should we put on the shopping bags? Needs to be unique so it gets people's attention. It's about you, girlfriend. What says 'Emily Kincaid' more than anything else?"

"I don't know. A cane? Yoga pants with a fat knee and some extra pounds stuck in them?"

"Come on. You're not trying. Like Kim at Meadowbrooke said, you're supposed to be thinking positive, right? What's the most positive image you can think of from the last few months?"

Of course! The blond girl on a hill of daisies. It was the dream I'd had when I was in the hospital, and ever since, whenever I thought of the scene, it made me feel peaceful. It suddenly hit me that I had a physical picture of the scene.

"I have an idea. Let me find it to show you." I scanned the handwritten labels on the boxes stacked in the hall and started to root around. The girls helped me pull out the boxes labeled "Books," and I eventually found it—the poetry book from my childhood. I soon located *Afternoon on a Hill* by Edna St. Vincent Millay and the picture of the girl in the field of daisies.

"This." I pointed to the picture, unable to say more because of the emotions the illustration evoked.

Danielle looked doubtfully at the picture. "Okay. Can we copy it?"

"I don't think so, but I need something like this."

Danielle clapped her hands together. "Girls, this is exciting. I really have a good feeling about the idea."

Karly looked at the book again. "How are you going to get the picture made?"

"Well, I know a very talented graphic artist, and he owes me."

"You have *got* to be kidding me," Danielle exclaimed in disbelief.

"Good luck with that," said Karly. "Adam *is* very talented, but the laziest person I've ever met. No offense, Emily."

"None taken. Kidding about Adam. But I can barely draw stick people, and you two aren't much better."

They frowned.

I closed the book and slid it back into the box. "I know what. I'll use the drawing Matthew Singer did. It's darling." With some rifling through the stuff I had brought home from Meadowbrooke, I found Matthew's card with the childish drawing of a daisy.

"Aw. I remember this. He is the cutest little guy and obviously in love with you."

I leaned the card against the wall on a shelf. "I'll talk to him and Melissa about it. I think it will be fun, and Matthew will be happy about helping me."

"What are you going to name the shop?"

"*Emily's Dreams*," I said without hesitation. "But to set up a shop in my room…." I looked around doubtfully. "As small as it is, I'd need to use every square inch."

Karly frowned. "Emily. Not only would it be weird to have a shop in your bedroom, it's not realistic. You need a good location, so people can drop in when they see it. Who would suddenly think, 'Oh, I'll go shopping for used stuff in the Kincaid's back room?' and drive out here and knock on the door? What would be ideal is a little space on the town square."

Danielle sighed and dropped onto my bed. "Killjoy. But I have to admit you're right."

I didn't want to lose the enthusiasm. "I still think the idea is great. Last time I noticed, there were some empty spots on the Square, but I can afford to pay about zero in rent."

"What about Carla Standish? Isn't she a friend of your family? She has that awesome dress shop."

"I don't think second hand stuff would be a very good match with Carla's clientele, do you? Even if she had the extra space to offer."

Danielle was wearing her stubborn look. "I refuse to give up on *Emily's Dreams*. There has to be a way to make this happen."

Mom invited the girls to dinner, which was fun for all of us—even Hannah and Taylor.

Danielle helped herself to salmon patties, vegetables, and potatoes, and cleared her throat importantly. "I wonder if you all might have suggestions where we could set up a little shop for Emily."

I groaned, not quite ready to spring the idea on the fam.

"Shop?" Mom and Dad chorused.

"Yes," said Danielle. "To sell her extra stuff. Kind of an indoor yard sale, but classier."

"Seriously." Taylor rolled her eyes and looked to Hannah for agreement.

Hannah leaned around her twin so she could address Danielle more directly. "I think it sounds like fun."

I could only stare at her.

Hannah gestured to all of us in turn with her fork. "No, really. Why not? Most of Emily's things are in almost perfect condition. I mean, not the best taste, and the clothes are outdated, but in good shape. People around here don't have loads of money, and there's no second-hand shop. Just Carla Standish's dress shop, which is fabulous if you have the bucks, and stuff made in China that you can get at the dollar stores. I have clothes and shoes and handbags you could sell too. I'd want part of the money, of course."

"Well, sure," I agreed, shocked by Hannah's interest.

"A consignment shop," Mom said. "That *is* a good idea. I have clothes and maybe some housewares to put in it too." She batted her eyelashes at Dad. "Marcus?"

Dad's stubborn look appeared. "No. Absolutely not. I will build shelves, haul merchandise, even run a cash register on my days off, but I'm not looking to get rid of my possessions."

"Okay, okay, honey." She reached over and stroked his hand briefly. "Just asking. So where to put it?"

Dad looked relieved at the quick out and concentrated again on his food. "Maybe Darlene would let you use that building she bought and rehabbed. Temporarily, anyway. You could call her, Emily."

This was news. "Darlene? Aunt Darlene bought a building?"

"Yes. Well, it was while you were in the hospital, I

believe. I hadn't thought to mention it. That little building on the southwest corner of the Square. Used to be a children's clothing store back in the day?"

I nodded, knowing which one he meant. "It's tiny."

"It's narrow, but has more square footage than you'd think. I walked through it with Jamison one day after lunch. There are lots of shelves and drawers, a really nice setup for a shop. Darlene talked about making it a satellite of her Mendacious store or just renting it out. So far, it's fixed up but empty."

Mom sipped her tea, and spoke over the edge of the cup. "Her store is only twenty miles away. Why does she need a satellite?"

"I don't know. It was Darlene's idea, not mine. And not Jamison's but, of course, husbands aren't always consulted." He cleared his throat. Dad and his brother, my Uncle Jamison, are tight. "So anyway, you could call and ask her about it, Emily. The worst she can say is no."

Knowing Aunt Darlene, I was aware she could make 'no' very unpleasant, but also that if she liked my idea, she'd throw her support behind it without reservation. My mother liked to say she was a strong personality. It was kind of her, I think.

Danielle spoke up. "You need to ask her in person.

It's too easy to turn somebody down over the phone. Go see her and be sure to limp as much as possible. Playing the sympathy card never hurt."

"You can't sway my Aunt Darlene with common stunts like that. I'll call and tell her what we have in mind and see what she says."

Dad nodded, but Mom looked uncertain.

"It's a creative idea, and Aunt Darlene is all about thinking outside the box," said Hannah. "I think she'll do it." That was a good point. Aunt Darlene had a thriving interior design business in an area that all of us under-60s considered the Middle of Nowhere, Indiana.

Turns out, Hannah was right. Aunt Darlene was nearly as enthusiastic about the idea as the girls and I were. I was glad I had called instead of visiting her, because Aunt Darlene's energy was wearing me out even via the phone.

"I'll pick you up tomorrow when I get back to town, and you can see the little place. I think this will be just divine, Emily. I knew there was a good reason for me to buy that building. Jamison, of course, pooh-poohed it. Men can be tiring at times, Emily dear." She paused. "Oops. I shouldn't say that to you, should I, after that latest boyfriend ditched you? But hey, I'm sure you're better off without him."

"Yes, I am. Thanks."

"Excellent. We're all set." She turned up the sound on her TV in anticipation of hanging up. "I'll call when I leave Mendacious tomorrow."

"So?" Karly and Danielle asked anxiously when I ended the call.

"She's going to take me to see it tomorrow night. We haven't talked money yet, and I hesitated to bring it up. If it can't happen because of that, so be it. At least, I will have tried, right?"

They nodded.

"And I'll have spent time with Aunt Darlene, which doesn't happen often. She's always busy."

"And you'll get to ride in her Mercedes."

I shrugged, laughing. "Definitely don't mind that."

***

The ride in the Mercedes was awesome, and the shop was ideal. I loved it immediately.

"Wow, Aunt Darlene. This is a great little space."

She stood in the center of the room and slowly gazed around her domain. "All the shelving, drawers, mirrors, and dressing rooms were already here. We had to update, rip up the nasty carpet, and rescue the hardwood floor. And clean. There's lots of storage in the back too. I'm not sure what to do with the space, honestly." She turned to me. "Tell me more about your idea."

"A consignment shop. I have so much stuff of my own to sell, and Hannah mentioned people in Serendipity might really support a second-hand shop if the merchandise is in good shape and the price is right. It started out as just a way to pare down my belongings. Mom calls it 'downsizing.'"

"Is that right? What an unusual endeavor for someone your age. I hear it is becoming popular to get rid of all your belongings and travel the world with just a backpack." She looked amused by the idea. "Is that what you're planning, Emily? How exciting."

"No—not really. Just getting rid of things I don't use, but someone else might want." I paused, forcing myself to bring up the dreaded topic of money. "Plus I can use some income. I need to pay my parents back, and I'd like to get my own place soon."

"Admirable reasons, dear." She walked away and gazed out at our castle-like courthouse through one of the empty display windows. I held my breath, fearing what she might say.

Finally she broke the silence. "I tell you what.

Since I don't have an immediate plan for this space, if you want to set up your little shop for the time being, put up a tasteful sign, I'm open to that. You can pay the utilities, but I won't charge rent. I can't imagine utilities would be too high."

I hoped not. "Wow. Thanks. That would be great." If I'd been talking to Uncle Jamison, I would have hugged him, but Aunt Darlene—you're always afraid of wrinkling her clothes or mussing her perfect hair. We shook on it.

Chapter Fourteen

Preparations for the shop got underway. The girls and I made color copies of Matthew's new drawing, with my name on the top, the daisy in the middle, and "Dreams" under the daisy. We bought cheap gift bags from a dollar store and put a logo on each with rubber cement.

"I think you'll be busy," Danielle said as we worked. "People in town want to help you and your family after everything you've been through."

I shrugged. "You're probably right. It's one facet of living in Serendipity you can't fault. I mean, this town is as boring as cold oatmeal, but people really do care about each other."

Dad dug a board out of the garage, I painted it white, and the girls and I re-created Matthew's art work onto it. Luckily, we were copying the work of a four year old, because none of us was much better than that, skill-wise. When the sign was done, and we got Aunt Darlene's okay on it, Dad and Uncle Jamison hung it on the building. One night Dad brought me a small plastic sign from the hardware store that said "Open" on one side. On the other side, it said "We will return at…" and a picture of a clock with little hands you could move.

My parents, the twins, Danielle and Karly, and Uncle Jamison all helped move stuff into the building, and I spent a day setting up my little shop.

That night I was happily exhausted. As I lay in bed reading, Mom knocked on my door and came in. She sat on the edge of my bed, looking worried. "Your shop is a fun idea, sweetie. I just hope you won't be disappointed if people don't show up."

I knew her concern was for me. "We'll see. I think it'll be okay, Mom."

"All right, Emily. Just saying…."

The sign in the shop window said, "We will return at…9:00." I meant to be ready for customers on time tomorrow morning—Friday. I hoped at the end of the day I would need to fill some empty spaces on the shelves.

Mom drove me to town. "Do you want me to come

in and help?" She was really offering to keep me company on a very long, boring day.

"No thanks, Mom. I'm good." She had insisted on packing me a huge lunch, so I was set for the duration. "I promise to sit down when I can and call if I have any problems." I squeezed her hand. "I'll be okay, Mom." I climbed out with little difficulty and waved at her as she watched me flip the sign to "Open." As she pulled into the morning traffic, my first customer was approaching.

"Hey, Carla." Carla Standish was a dress designer who had a shop on the opposite side of the square but did most of her business online.

"Hey yourself, Emily." She gave me a gentle hug. "I've been dying to see you again but didn't want to be a bother. Mom and Melissa kept me updated." She pulled off leather gloves and tucked them into the pockets of her perfect-fitting leather jacket. Her thick, black hair was pulled into a bun at the base of her neck and her makeup was so skillfully applied it didn't look as if she was wearing any. In my opinion, Carla didn't look like someone who'd been a lifelong resident of Serendipity, Indiana.

"Take your time and see if there's anything you like." I gestured all around the room. "*Emily's Dreams*, a hodgepodge of twenty-five years of accidental collecting."

She laughed and started to browse. "I don't really need anything. You know how it is."

"Yes I do. That's why I'm selling most of what I have."

She nodded. "Good point." She reached out a manicured hand and picked up a vase, turned it around, and examined it. "This is sweet. So delicate."

I watched her, remembering the boy who had given it to me. "Probably a miracle it hasn't been broken, really."

"How much do you want for it, Emily?"

I quoted her a price and she shook her head. "Please. It's worth more than that." She handed me ten times what I had stated, and when I would have protested, she wrapped my fingers around the bills. "This is what I'm paying and not a penny less. Okay?"

Tears gathered in my eyes. I knew her generosity stemmed from really caring about me and the fam and that refusing would be ungrateful. "Okay. Let me wrap it for you." The girls and I had bought some packages of tissue paper at the dollar store, but I also added wadded-up newspaper to make sure it would be safe in the bag. I started to hand it to Carla, but drew the bag back, my attention suddenly caught by a glint of morning light reflecting off one of the items on a shelf near the display window. "That's funny," I said and walked over to it. The item was a turquoise, ceramic ring holder I'd made in middle school art class. As I held it, I had a strong feeling that I should give it to Carla. It was weird, but I just knew that's what needed to happen. I wrapped it in tissue and slid it into the bag before turning back toward her. "Sorry. I lost my focus for a minute there." I held out the bag to her, and she took it, looking pleased.

"There's a little something extra inside for you," I said. "It's not worth anything—just a thank-you." I hugged her. "I appreciate you being my first customer, Carla."

"Wouldn't have missed it. I'm off to open my store now. Friday is sometimes a busy shopping day in town. You never know. Give me a shout if you need anything, okay?" She handed me a card with her shop's name— *Creations*—and phone number. On the back, she'd written her cell number too. She raised the bag and examined it. "I love your logo and shop name. It's just perfect. Much luck, honey!"

As she went out, someone else came in. It was like that all morning—a steady flow of people I knew, buying dust-catchers they said they loved and insisting on paying more than the quoted price. It wasn't always ten times as much, like Carla had done, but nobody agreed to pay *just* what I said the price was. Quite often, I slid a little something extra into the bag.

Dean and Alice Williams came in together just after noon.

"Hi. How are you guys?"

They both hugged me. "Fine. We're just fine, Emily. So glad to have you back in town and doing okay." Dean put his arm around Alice. "We talked about visiting you at that rehab place, but figured you needed to rest when they weren't working you." Alice nodded.

"That's okay. They worked me pretty hard, for sure. It was worth it, now that I'm moving around so much better." I gestured with Lighting. "Look around and see if there's anything you like. Still loads of stuff, and this is just the first time filling the shelves."

"Oh, my." Alice's eyes grew wide. "Really?"

"I know, right? I'm not a hundred percent sure how I managed to accumulate so much."

Alice glanced toward Dean, whose back was turned, and winked at me. "Some of us come by the habit of acquisitiveness quite naturally."

Dean turned around, brows raised. "Some of us whose initials might be DW?" He laughed. "I can take a little constructive criticism. And I won't even mention my beautiful wife's collection of retro kitchen…*stuff.*"

Alice held up a hand. "Okay, okay. Truce."

Dean was a local barber and Alice worked for a lawyer in Serendipity. Once or twice Alice picked up an item and showed it to Dean, saying, "Honey, you know what this reminds me of?" He didn't always get it right away, and she would tell a brief story of a trip they had taken or some other event in their life. Pretty cool couple, though I had never known them well.

Dean picked up an ugly ash tray that said *Jones & Co.* on it. "You're getting rid of a family heirloom, Emily?" *Jones & Co* is where my dad and Uncle Jamison work. Aunt Darlene's dad actually owns it, I think.

I dismissed it with a gesture. "Ha. There are like a million of those in town from back in the 1960s, I think. Well, maybe not a million but too many. So, yes. Wrap it up for you?" I grabbed a bag as a joke.

"Yes. I'll take it." Dean walked over and handed it to me. Alice set down the stack of blank books she'd been looking at and came over to see what we'd been discussing.

"Oh, please. And the reason we need a *Jones & Co.* ashtray is what?"

"Just a reminder." Dean said smugly, and Alice

blushed a little.

"How much is it, Emily?" He pulled out his wallet and had it open, ready to lay out the money. I quoted a price I thought was reasonable because the ashtray could at least be used to drop paper clips in or something.

"No way," said Dean, and he gave me a much bigger bill.

"Um. Wow. Really?" Every time it happened, this surprised me.

"Take it, Emily," Alice said softly. "It's kind of a piece of our history. Not that I think we actually need a reminder." She gave Dean a look, but he was beaming, looking at the dumb ash tray. You'd have thought he had just won a race and this was the trophy.

"Okay. Thanks a *lot*, guys." I put some tissue around the ashtray and some newspaper for good measure. "Um, Alice, I noticed you looking at the blank books a minute ago. Did you want some of those?"

"I love them, but I have dozens at home. Can't generally stop myself from buying them. At this point I'm not sure I have space for even one more in a drawer."

Dean looked relieved.

I went to the shelf by the books and picked up a vintage fountain pen and came back. "This pen is great if you like to hand write a lot. It's just not something I enjoy to be honest. Especially fountain pens. Too messy."

Alice took the pen and tested the way it felt in her hand. "It's beautiful, Emily. I used to have one and loved writing with it." She looked at me, her face beaming. "How much?"

"Nothing. This item free with purchase, as they say." I frowned, locking eyes with her. "That's the only way you're getting it, Alice. I want you to have it, okay?"

Dean and Alice exchanged looks. She said, "No. I love it, but someone else will pay money for it, and you would be better off."

Dean shook his head. "Alice, nobody else in Serendipity is going to want an old-fashioned fountain pen. If you leave it here, Emily keeps it, which is fine."

I shook my head. "I don't want it, which is why it's on the shelf."

Alice held up her hands, one of which held the pen. "All right. All right. Thank you so much, Emily. I'll think of you every time I use it."

"Oh gosh, don't do that. Just enjoy. Write

something awesome with it." She handed me the pen, and I wrapped it in a little piece of tissue because the item seemed so special to her. I slid it gently into the bag.

Dean took the bag and Alice hugged me. "Thanks, Emily," she said. "You've made both our days."

At five o'clock, I was wiped out and relieved to flip the sign to *Closed*.

Mom pulled up at the curb, parked, and came in. "How was the first day for *Emily's Dreams*, sweetie?"

"Amazing. People spent a lot of money. Well, they gave me a lot. Everybody overpaid and seemed thrilled about doing it."

"That's our friends and neighbors. A very generous bunch. So, are you adding an Emily Kincaid wing onto the library soon?"

Mom helped me turn off lights, and when I had locked up, I was glad to sink into the seat of her van and massage my leg on the ride home. When we got there, I showed her the box I was keeping the money in. She started sorting it by denominations of bills. "Oh, my. More generous than I imagined. This is very nice."

"I want to pay you and Dad back for all you've been through."

"Sweetie, you don't have to pay us. You've got a medical deductible and a deductible on the car. After that, whatever you make off your little store is yours to keep."

"I can start paying my premiums instead of you guys covering them like you've done since the wreck."

"Yes. That would be helpful." Having sorted and straightened, she returned the money to the box and closed the lid. "Well, you're doing wonderfully. I must say I'm surprised."

I slid the box onto a shelf by my bed. "Can I help with dinner? Lunch was great, but now that I smell dinner, I'm starving."

She laughed. "I'm glad you're hungry. I've got a roast and vegetables in the crock pot, and bread just out of the oven. But we need to wait 'til your father gets home. The twins have dates. They've been primping for hours."

"Poor Mom. You never get a break, do you? Between me and the twins, I mean. I imagine we drive you crazy."

She hugged me. "Not *that* crazy. Besides, what would I do without you? I love the energy and enthusiasm you girls have. It makes me feel young too."

"What will you do when we're all gone?"

Her face immediately changed from happiness to desolation. "I don't like to think about that."

"But, Mom, it's happening pretty soon, you know. I hope to get my own place before long, and the twins leave in the fall. You know?"

"Of course. Yes, I know that. It's what parents raise their children to do. Little birds leaving the nest and all that." She sighed. "It will sure be different here with just Dad and me in the house. Goodness. I'll have to learn to cook for just two people." Her brief laugh sounded hollow.

"So where is Dad?"

"At work. They were behind on some important orders, so the factory worked late today." She looked at her watch and frowned. "He should be here soon."

"Oh—that reminds me. Dean Williams bought an old *Jones & Co.* ashtray from me, and I'm pretty sure he doesn't even smoke."

"That's funny. I don't think he does."

"He had this kind of smug look and said something about it being a reminder. I dunno. It was an inside joke with him and Alice."

"Well, it might have been something to do with Alice marrying Dean and not Jamison."

"What?"

She nodded. "Through most of high school, Alice dated your Uncle Jamison. They made a beautiful couple. But…well, things happened. Jamison hooked up with Darlene, and Alice started to date Dean. You were so young when it happened I'm not surprised you don't remember. I thought that, like typical rebound relationships, they wouldn't last, but look at them—all four of them. They've been married a lot of years and seem happy, don't they?"

I squeezed my eyes shut trying to picture it. "Okay, it's just weird to think of Uncle Jamison dating Alice. I guess because I don't remember before he was with Aunt Darlene, and I never really thought…."

"You never thought we old people had a life prior to our current, boring marriage-and-kids stuff." She nodded. "I know what you mean. I was the same way at your age. You'll have this same conversation with your own daughter someday."

"Huh. I don't know about that. Maybe the marriage-and-kids stuff isn't for me."

"Why do you say that?"

"Well, no prospects right now, and I'm already

twenty-five."

She laughed—a genuine one this time, and bigger than I'd heard from her in a long time. "Oh, Emily. I don't think you're past it quite yet. What about David Standish, for instance?"

"Oh, Mom. He's so much older. And he's not interested in me that way."

"Hmm. Yet he took flowers to you at Meadowbrooke and invited himself for dinner when you got home from there. It's fairly obvious to me he's interested."

I shook my head. "Probably your lasagna brought him here, not me."

"You think he smelled lasagna in the oven from miles away and found your dad so he could eat with us?"

"Maybe. Men like to eat. Look at Ben."

She refused to leave the topic. "I'm reasonably sure David is interested in you, Emily. Granted I didn't see it coming—"

I shook my head. "I don't know…." I remembered the kisses quite well, but that was just the one time. I hadn't told anyone about it, not even Karly and Danielle. Like the dream of the girl on the hill, that kiss by the river was my secret. Well, the kiss was a secret I shared with David if, in fact, he even cared. After that night, he hadn't exactly been a regular visitor to the lockup, as I would expect a guy to do if he was interested in a girl. David's life as a player of the field was well documented, and I had seen the documentation over the years of cleaning his house. How dumb would it be for me to expect more from him than maybe to have my little job back? Worst case, he might break my heart and find someone else to clean his house.

But Mom was on a roll now. "Plus in these days, you don't have to wait 'til marriage to have a child. I'd think it would be much more difficult to raise a child or children alone, but it's an option. Look at Melissa Singer for instance. She's a wonderful example of a single mother."

"She sure is." But I knew from my days of being in their home how hard Melissa worked building her career and making sure little Matthew was taken care of the way she wanted him to be.

"And there's nothing to say you have to do any of it. Once you get your life on track, you might find that being single and on your own is the best lifestyle for you."

"I think I need to try it for a while at least. I've never even lived alone."

She nodded. "You'll figure it out."

"I have to say I'm glad you didn't choose any of those other options, Mom. Especially the part about not having kids."

She grinned, getting the meaning. "I'm happy that pleases you, sweetie. It's important to be thankful for life, even if it isn't the life we think we want."

We heard the garage door behind the house open, and our focus shifted in that direction. Dad was home, thank goodness, and this conversation could end.

Mom stood up. "We can take up the topic again at dinner, if you like."

"No thanks."

I was pretty sure she was kidding, but still.

Chapter Fifteen

Sunday afternoon, Gran picked me up for our trip to Lillian Standish's. It was a treat to leave the house for a while, and with it, the drama of the twins, plus worrying about how Mom and Dad would handle empty nesting. I sighed, leaning against the headrest of Gran's big black sedan as it glided along the highway.

"It's nice to have you to myself, honey." She kept her eyes on the road, but her voice was sincere.

"Same here, Gran. Thanks for rescuing me." I laughed hollowly. "I shouldn't joke. Mom and Dad have been awesome to me...better than I deserve for sure."

"But it's hard on you not being able to get out and go whenever you want to."

"Yes. Very hard, but I know there's no way I

would be a safe driver right now. My reaction time would be super slow."

"Try to be patient. I know without a doubt that in time, everything will work out for you."

The future looked more foggy than sunny to me, but Gran's outlook was similar to Kim's, the aide I now realized I missed. "I hope you're right."

"I usually am," she said, flicking up her right turn indicator. "Emily, you keep doing your exercises, and you'll become physically stronger. Do the other work you have on your heart, and that will make even more difference for your future."

Goosebumps immediately appeared on my arms at what she had said. I'd always felt like Grandma Reba had a sixth sense.

"Gran, I don't know there's so much on my heart except to get rid of a bunch of stuff. Kind of a strange objective for someone my age. Everybody seems to agree about that."

"I think it's wonderful, honey. And look how well you're doing with it. I've heard from several people how much they enjoyed visiting *Emily's Dreams*. It gives your friends and neighbors a way to help you and visit without feeling they're a bother. Your accident, and how badly hurt you were, seemed to tear a little hole in our community. The shop is helping repair that as you heal along with it." She shook her head. "In a close-knit community like ours, tragedy hurts everyone. Being able to physically help makes all the difference."

I shook my head, trying to take in all that. "You really think my shop is a help to Serendipity, not just to me?"

"I would say so. Yes. It's not all about you, Emily Elizabeth. Nothing in your life is *only* about you. All of us are connected and yearn for opportunities to share each other's burdens as well as happiness."

That made sense. I guess that's why we throw parties for birthdays and weddings and have long lines at funeral visitations. We need those times in order to remain a community. My little shop seems to be serving a good purpose and that made me happy.

She turned again, and we were on Tree Farm Road. In spite of the brown grass of winter, when the Christmas tree farm came into sight, the hills of stately evergreen trees made me happy, as always.

"I'm glad to come out here again. It's been too long." I pictured David standing in front of his house on one of the hills further back on the farm. As we slowed for the turn into the drive, I dragged my brain away from David, to the purpose of our visit. "Um...Lillian's doing well now, isn't she?"

Gran slowed even more to take the gravel lane comfortably. "Lillian is a strong woman and will be fine. Widowhood is a hard way to live and a hurt that never goes away. Now that she's alone in the house where she and Harry spent their long marriage, it's yet another adjustment. I'm sure it's also an adjustment for Francie and her husband, being back together after so many months." She made a slight *tsking* sound.

"What? You think Francie shouldn't have stayed so long?"

"That was a decision for them to make. I just hope all is well with Francie and Brad. Too many marriages end in divorce these days." She cut the engine and pulled the keys. "Marriage, Emily, is not easy. A good one is like a good garden. You don't just throw seeds in the dirt when spring arrives and expect a bountiful harvest in the fall. Many say marriage is hard work, but I think of it as tending the garden. You reap what you sow. That's the kind of marriage Lillian and Harry had—and the kind your grandfather and I had." She paused and I thought she was going to say something about my parents' marriage which I thought looked pretty healthy. "As with anything, you get out of it what you put in."

I held up my hands. "Hey, Gran, I'm not looking at getting married. I mean, maybe I deserve a lecture on relationships, but at this moment, it's kind of pointless since I don't have one."

As for the breakup with Adam, the less said the better. I tried to pretend he didn't exist and had never been in my life. I dreaded meeting up with him in town. In a small place like Serendipity, there was no way you could avoid running into people again unless they died or moved away and never came back. I didn't wish death on him but wouldn't mind if he found a new life on a different continent. I definitely wasn't at the point with Adam that Kim Rose was with her ex-boyfriend.

Gran smiled. "Oh, honey, your new relationship will make all the difference, if you decide to let it."

I clamped my mouth shut, refusing to be drawn further. If she was talking about David, she was getting way ahead of reality.

Gran parked the car in front of Lillian's house and hurried to my side of the car, ready to steady me, if needed. Daisy, Lillian's happy dog, eagerly greeted us. I petted her silky head.

"Thanks, Gran. I'm good."

"I'm always ready to help, Emily. You know that." She slung her purse onto one shoulder so she'd have both hands free in case I looked ready to fall or something. "We can pick up this topic later."

I sincerely hoped not.

Lillian Standish came out onto her front porch and down the steps. "Hello. It's wonderful to see you both." She fell into step next to me.

Oh, the craziness of being hovered over by these two ladies. I was proud to maneuver the three steps up to the porch without help except from the sturdy wooden railing. At the top, Lightning and I were steady, and I heard a soft sigh of relief from Gran. It was a big accomplishment. Each one made me feel stronger.

The love seat that Lillian had told me about before had been brought down from the attic and was in the living room. The curved wood legs and brocade upholstery were classic and feminine.

"Oh, Lillian. I love it."

Lillian ran a hand along the rich wood at the top edge. "Good. You can use it as long as you like. Bring it back when you're done. I'll have one of the boys deliver it to your parents' house."

"Wonderful. And when I get my own place, should I bring it back?"

"Not at all. It's yours to use, Emily. I'm just not ready to get rid of it forever. It's a family piece, but so far none of my children want it in their homes."

I agreed to her requirement about the love seat, and Lillian led us into the dining room where the computer had been set up on the table.

"I told Jim to put it here. We only use this table a few times a year, and if the computer is in the way, we can put it on the sideboard or on the floor. Jim thought maybe I'd want it on Harry's desk, but I decided against it. Harry would turn in his grave to have a computer in his office." She smiled, love in her eyes but not anguish. I remembered seeing her at the funeral visitation for Harry last year, the grief so strong my chest hurt to look at her. She had definitely made a lot of progress.

Lillian pulled out a chair for me. Evidently Jim was somewhat knowledgeable, because the cords were all connected. I sat down and pushed the button to boot up the system. Since it wasn't exactly the newest model, this took a little while. Adam had pronounced it too old to be of any use when I'd unpacked it at the apartment he and I shared. He'd had a new desktop that he used for online gaming, and it was light years faster than mine. Not that he ever let me use it, of course. The more I looked back on that relationship, the more I realized it had been doomed from the beginning.

Lillian disappeared into the kitchen and came back with a big plate of chocolate chip cookies. My mouth started to water.

She set the plate on the table next to me. "We have to keep up our strength. Coffee will be ready in a few minutes.

I'd brought a small, blank notebook from my collection. "You can use this, Lillian, to record your passwords. Eventually, you might want to get a little address book and alphabetically list the websites you visit, and your username and password for each."

She looked dumbstruck, and I stopped and set the notebook and pen on the table. "We'll deal with that when it comes up. What would you like to be able to do online?"

A couple of hours flew by. Lillian, like Gran, was interested in lots of topics. I got her set up in a couple of social media sites and made bookmarks for those and for some on-line stores and a news aggregator.

"Emily, this is wonderful. I can't tell you how happy I am." Lillian gave me a quick hug, but when she offered the cookie plate again, I forced myself to decline.

"Lillian, it's good you're a quick learner, or I'd be too wide to fit through your door on the way out." I gestured to my physique. "I'm getting rounder by the day as it is. I need more exercise and less food, instead of the other way around."

She chuckled. "What can I pay you, Emily? For the computer and today's lesson, I mean."

"Oh, nothing. I hadn't even considered it. I'm glad for you to have the computer. It's getting some age on it, so if you find you enjoy having one, you may want to upgrade to something faster."

Lillian was unconvinced. "I need to feel right about this, dear. Plus, I'm sure I'll have more questions."

I hugged her. "You're doing me a favor with the love seat, plus giving my old computer a new home. Helping you learn a little about it was fun for me. I'm available for future consultations at the price of a cookie an hour. How does that sound?"

She gently patted the top of the monitor. "Very reasonable."

"Great. That's settled. I'm available anytime by phone and in person, as long as Gran can bring me."

There were a couple of knocks on the door and it swung open.

Jim Standish wiped his shoes carefully on the mat before walking over to kiss his mother's cheek. He shook hands with Gran and me. "Did I get here in time to sit in on the lesson? Great to see you, Emily. You're looking well." He leaned closer and whispered loudly. "Running with kind of a fast crowd here, aren't you?' He shook his head and tried to look serious.

Lillian huffed. "Watch your mouth, son, or I'll

unfriend you."

Jim looked from her to Gran and then to me. I felt color rush into my cheeks but couldn't help a grin. "We worked a little bit on social media, Jim."

He threw his head back and laughed. "You can't unfriend me, Mom. I'm not on any of that stuff. If I started, I'd be asked for free, online, legal consultations, 24/7." He shook his head. "Better to keep my computer at work and my private life...private."

"Well spoken, son. I'm sure Melissa would agree."

"It's wonderful you and Melissa are together again, Jim," Gran enthused. "I knew that would happen."

Lillian nodded. "Yes. We just didn't know when or how."

He looked from one to the other, an eyebrow raised in disbelief. "You did, eh? I sure wish one of you had told me."

"Jim, we couldn't have done that." Gran shook her head. "And if we had, you wouldn't have believed us."

"You two are what—psychic?"

They shrugged in unison, and Lillian said, "We've been best friends for more decades than we'd care to admit. We finish each other's sentences and know each other's deepest secrets. What hurts me, hurts Reba and vice versa. Isn't that right, Reba?"

Gran nodded slowly.

Amused, Jim leaned toward me. "See what I mean? Not the kind of crowd you should be running with, Emily. Entirely too wild and *out there*." He stepped back. "Just wanted to come in, say hello, get my ears pinned back, and see if there's anything you need from me, Mom."

She shook her head. "I'm fine, son. Emily likes the love seat, so you can make arrangements to deliver it to her soon. But for now, you go on and have a nice evening with Melissa and Matthew." A brow raised. "Unless the two of you have decided to let him stay here while you go out."

"No, we're good. Thanks, Mom. After all, I've missed out on four years of Matthew's life." He snagged a cookie and bit off half of it. "We're just eating carryout pizza and playing board games tonight. Should be a hoot. You're still on for next Saturday afternoon, right?"

She brightened. "Absolutely. I look forward to having Matthew here for a few hours. He makes me feel so alive."

I shifted in my chair, uncomfortable after being in

one place for so long. "He's a sweetheart. I had a lot of fun staying with Matthew."

Lillian touched my hand. "They miss you."

"Yes. Melissa brought him to Meadowbrooke to visit me a couple of times." I didn't say they had invited me to move in with them.

Gran nodded. "Just think—if Melissa hadn't suddenly needed another babysitter, who knows how long it would have taken for Melissa and Jim to get back together."

I hadn't thought about it quite that way. "The wreck took me out of the picture, Lillian stepped in, and..." I glanced at Lillian, who nodded enigmatically. My goose bumps reappeared.

Gran sipped her coffee, closely watching my face. "When you believe in Love, it's easier to see that coincidences are often more than that."

Jim scooped up a few cookies and slid them into his coat pocket. Patting it gently, he said, "Just in case the truck breaks down on the way and I need nourishment."

The door closed behind him. Lillian and Gran shared a secret look, and one of them hummed as they tidied up the dining table, clearing away the notes from our lesson as well as Jim's cookie crumbs. Something was up here, and no one seemed inclined to enlighten me.

"You still babysit Matthew once in a while, Lillian?"

She looked at me. "Yes, as you say, once in a while. Matthew goes to preschool and daycare now. Melissa took that step when Christmas tree season got into full swing, worried that watching over him and taking care of the Christmas shop would be too much for me. She decided it was important for Matthew to be acclimated to this new schedule, because he'll be in kindergarten in the fall." Lillian sighed. "Amazing. By the time he's in kindergarten, almost a year will have passed since Melissa bought the old Osborne house on North Main and moved back to Serendipity. So many aspects of life have changed for us in a short time."

When Gran and I started back toward Tree Farm Road, I thought of traveling up and down this driveway so many times in my life, to do my weekly job of cleaning David's house. He'd said he was holding it open for me, but how long would that last? My babysitting job was gone for good, and we all understood that my shop was temporary. In fact, everything in my life felt temporary.

"Gran, it freaks me out to think that my wreck set events into motion in other people's lives. You and Lillian say you already knew Melissa and Jim would get together. But as the person whose wreck was the catalyst for that…I'm starting to feel like I have no control over my life."

She stopped at the end of the drive, before pulling onto Tree Farm Road, and faced me. "Honey, matters will take their course. If you do something to alter the course, that may only delay the inevitable. Melissa and Jim would have gotten together without your wreck but not as soon. That might have changed something else on down the line. There is a lot of daily cause and effect we're unaware of with those we know and even with complete strangers."

I thought about that. "Okay. I guess I can sort of see what you're saying. I sure hope I don't have to do anything so drastic next time I'm a catalyst."

"I believe your shop is something special, Emily Elizabeth. It's also one of the most unselfish projects I've ever seen you do. I see lots of good coming out of your recent decisions."

I sighed and relaxed a bit. "Thanks, Gran. That means a lot."

Chapter Sixteen

Gran invited me to have dinner with her, which was another nice change from my new normal. I washed and cut vegetables for the salad. Gran whipped up a casserole and after sliding it into the preheated oven came to stand by me while I worked.

"Emily, before I take you home, I want you to see what I have downstairs."

"Ooh. That's mysterious, Gran. Give me a hint?"

"It might make your parents happy, and it's something your Grandpa Geoffrey set in motion many years ago."

"Oka-ay. In other words, no *helpful* hints. Got it."

Dinner was yummy, but the best part about it was Gran's company. She always had so many interesting topics to discuss. When we finished, and thank goodness dessert was fruit instead of something fattening, we cleared the table together. I stifled a yawn.

"It's been a big day, Emily. Are you ready to go home by way of the surprise downstairs?"

Oh boy. Unless it was a pile of money, I wasn't sure I could manage much enthusiasm. "Okay. I faked that yawn so I could see the surprise, you know."

She winked. "Of course, you did."

In order to make the unveiling easier and safer, we put on our coats, got in her car, and she drove around to the lower level driveway. I sure didn't want to tumble down her stairs and have a setback we'd all regret.

As we got out of her car, I said, "Now let's see what you've got chained in the basement, Gran."

She led the way to the half-glass door, unlocked it and stepping inside, switched on the light.

I took a deep breath as I crossed the threshold. "Wow. Gran, it's beautiful." Her basement was now an apartment, kitchen on the right, dining and living areas combined. There were two good-sized bedrooms, and the bathroom was way bigger than the one I was using as my own right now. It was so light and inviting and modern looking that it could have been in New York City instead of little Serendipity, Indiana.

She laughed that musical laugh I'd heard my whole life that always made me feel happy and loved. "Your parents think my house is too big for me, so I'm proving them wrong. It didn't take the contractor too much time to do this because the plumbing was already here. Geoffrey and I had this apartment idea in mind as a possible eventuality when we built the house." She looked at me, her enthusiasm evident. "How would you like to be the first to live down here? If you need something, I'm within earshot. If you need something I can't do, we're in town so help is readily available. Of course, it isn't fancy." She looked at the big room again, and I could tell she was pleased with how it had turned out.

"It's so pretty." I sighed. "But Gran, I don't think this is it. I don't want to sound ungrateful—"

"Oh, honey. You've been through so much. First the hospital, then Meadowbrooke, then—"

I cut her off, not wanting sympathy. "Don't be concerned about me and Adam."

"I'm not concerned about Adam at all. He has to figure out his own path, poor boy. And I don't exactly worry about you. I thought this place might be one where you could find peace and think about what happens next for you." She was frowning, and Grandma Reba seldom frowned.

I took her hand. "I'm not sure what happens next, but I'm good where I am right now. If this had been ready when I first left Meadowbrooke, I probably would have said yes faster than you could offer it. Now that the little room at home has led to my shop, I feel like I'm doing something worthwhile. You helped me see that, Gran."

She squeezed my hand slightly. "I am glad. Well, I guess I'll put an ad in the paper."

"Yes. Somebody needs this place. It's really cool. Just be careful who you rent to."

She waved away my concern. "I'll be cautious. I didn't get to be this age without being able to look out for myself. I may specify that I'm looking for a widow. I think it might be just perfect."

"I bet it will, Gran. You're a great example and so strong." I cleared my throat. "Gran, how did you get over losing Grandpa Geoffrey?"

"Honey, you don't get over losing a spouse or family member. You eventually come to accept it, adjust to your new situation, and learn to live again. But you don't get over it."

"Oh." I didn't miss Adam anymore. That had sure been a short adjustment period and probably indicated I hadn't been as deeply in love as I thought.

"You'll eventually accept your losses, Emily. The difference between you and me is that most of your life is ahead of you. I have my memories, but you have so many memories yet to make."

Sure age was a difference, but the bigger, more important difference was that she had loved one time, deeply, with her whole being. I wasn't sure I'd ever been in love like that. The pain Gran had gone through had been heart-wrenching for all of us to watch, even as we were dealing with our own experience in losing Grandpa Geoffrey. Maybe being in love wasn't worth the inevitable pain when it ended.

That night in bed I thought about the pretty apartment in Gran's basement and hoped that some woman who was on her own after becoming a widow would find that place and make a new start on life there. It would be easier to make a new start in a house that wasn't full of memories, wouldn't it? Maybe that's why I wasn't drawn to the idea. I had hundreds of memories of that house, even of the basement back when the Standish kids and Ben and I were banished down there because we had too much energy and the weather outside was nasty. Yet the old summer kitchen didn't hold memories for me. It had always been a store room, and by converting it, we had, by mere chance, created a place where I could find the kind of peace Gran had spoken of. It was almost like accidentally finding an entirely new room in our house.

Or maybe it hadn't been an accident at all. I fell asleep wondering about which events in my life had seemed inconsequential at the time but had been important in the long run.

Chapter Seventeen

Turn the page, Emily.

I turned and scanned the room, knowing I was alone. It would be pretty difficult for anyone to hide in my little shop. Part of me had hoped the voice might stay at Meadowbrooke. I resolutely shrugged off the weirdness of the recurring nudge and continued to restock the shelves from the remaining boxes in the store room. Several townspeople came in each day and made purchases, usually insisting on overpaying. As often as not, I felt compelled to put something extra in the bag. It might be a strange way of running a shop, but mine was a strange kind of shop, created for a strange reason. The entire process had begun to feel perfect.

My phone played Karly's ring.

"Hey.   How's   Serendipity's   newest

businesswoman?"

I laughed. "I'm okay. Good."

"I love hearing that, Emily. Today is a follow-up with the doc, right?"

"Yep. Mom and I head out soon for that."

"Okay. Just wanted to make sure you'll let us know what happens, okay? Send a text on your way home or something. Danielle and I kind of have a bet on this."

"Kind of a bet?"

"We have a bet. There's a week's worth of dishwashing riding on it, so be sure you let us know."

"Got it." We hung up and I wondered what the girls expected Dr. Jay to tell me.

***

"You're doing well, Miss Emily," Dr. Jay pronounced with a bright smile after looking at me and writing on my chart. "How do you feel?"

"Pretty good. I'm still slow, but I get around. Sometimes I even do without Lightning." He chuckled, and I fiddled with the clipboard that was sitting on the small table between us.

He crossed his arms, leaning back in his chair.

"And what do you do to fill your time?"

"I sort of started a business. It's just a little shop where I'm selling stuff I don't need anymore."

"Oh, yes?" He looked at Mom too. She shook her head in disbelief and continued. "Emily is downsizing."

"Ah. Likely more than that," he said, nodding.

"What do you mean?" she and I asked at the same time.

He shrugged. "It seems to me that our Emily is shedding her cocoon and preparing to enter her life as a butterfly."

We stared at him, dumbstruck.

His smile widened. "I will be surprised if this is not so. But I will not know for a very long time." He sat forward, picked up the clipboard, and wrote something quickly. "Your need for frequent follow-ups is at an end. Please make an appointment to come back and see me in a year." He pointed to the doorknob where Lightning was hanging. "I think Lightning's time of usefulness in your life is nearly at an end, as well. You should only rely on that help when you are very tired. Your progress has been most admirable. Is it not surprising what one can do when one has a purpose in this life?"

I didn't mean to snort but couldn't help it. "Thanks for all the kind words, Dr. Jay, but I don't know what purpose you're talking about."

He didn't say anything to that, just told us goodbye, left the room, and went down the hall to meet with his next patient.

As soon as Mom pulled out of the medical complex parking lot, I called Karly and Danielle. Karly had expected Dr. Jay to say I didn't need to see him again for a year. Danielle had been more pessimistic, so Karly won the bet. I told them what Dr. Jay had said about me finding a purpose, but they were using speakerphone and were already fussing about the dishwashing by the time I got into that.

Mom and I rode the rest of the way home in silence, deep in our own thoughts.

That night I sent a text to Kimberly Rose, the nursing student from Meadowbrooke. I had only sent her an occasional text since I got home, and she had responded. But I felt like she was the person I needed to talk with. In spite of being busy with school and work, she said she would get with me and schedule a visit. I looked forward to it more than I had looked forward to anything in a long time. I wanted her to see what was going on in my new life and wanted to hear what she thought of my progress.

Chapter Eighteen

Gran looked at me cautiously as I stood on the sidewalk at the grocery. "You're sure you can manage, Emily Elizabeth?"

"Absolutely. Please, go ahead and do what you need to do. I'll be fine."

"Hmm." She tipped her head, concentrating and looking undecided. "I should be back in half an hour at the longest."

"I'm fine," I repeated. "Really. Take your time." We both knew I couldn't be hovered over forever. I had walked all the aisles of the *JayC* numerous times since my rehab—sometimes with Gran, sometimes to "help" Mom, a couple of times with Danielle and Karly to pick up junk food and gossip on the way to a gathering of friends from high school. Okay, that time with the girls hadn't been all the aisles, and to be honest, I did ride part of the time in the kiddie car/cart because we all found it hilarious until a manager caught us at it. But I knew I was up for this. Each day I felt the need to do more on my own. Getting myself ready for whatever happened after the shop was empty meant being in good enough physical condition that I could hold down a job and make a decent wage.

Gran seemed to convince herself of my ability. "All right. Half an hour and I will catch up with you, dear." I closed the car door and stepped further back on the sidewalk. Gran pulled away in her black sedan to do a couple of "walking errands" down on the town square. I hoped she would take her time and visit when she went into the stores instead of just hurrying back to me. Still, I was relieved to see someone had left a cart on the sidewalk. I did great in my little shop, where there was always something handy to grab hold of if I needed to steady myself, but the openness of the large grocery store could be a challenge. I pushed the cart in through the automatic doors, through the entryway to the produce and florist areas. The woman who did the flowers greeted me by name as I watched her create a pretty bouquet with roses and babies' breath.

I looked in the chilled case. "Do you have daisies?"

"Sure do, Emily. Want a bouquet?"

"Yes. It's a splurge, but it feels like winter is lasting forever, doesn't it?"

She grinned and whispered. "Nasty weather is good for business." I laughed at her honesty. She reached into the case and pulled out a big bunch of daisies. "Pick a vase, and we'll fix you up."

I found a simple one—short and squat, clear glass. She worked for a few minutes and I browsed at the other items ready to sell. A pretty display of paperwhite narcissus, pink and purple hyacinth, and some fat, red amaryllis.

She brought me the bouquet.

"Mmm. So pretty."

She nodded, and gestured at the plant display. "Thinking about something else too?"

I set the vase carefully in the child's seat portion of my cart. "This is it for me. The smell of those forced bulb flowers is amazing. I should buy some to do at home."

"Nothing perks up a space in winter like fresh flowers. They still have some narcissus bulbs at the hardware store, or did the last time I stopped in."

"Thanks. Maybe we can stop there on the way. Thanks for this too." I gently touched the vase. Makes my day." It was cheerful to have the bouquet in the cart as I shopped. I bought mostly basic stuff, the list carefully written by Gran. Fruits and veggies, a square loaf of sourdough bread, some stew meat, and other items for her week's menus.

She had found a renter for the basement apartment, a super nice lady who had been a widow for about six months and had just sold her home. Gran hired the same contractor to convert the second story of her house into another apartment, and the project was going well. It had been the most marvelous library all my life, but Gran had decided to keep some of the books on shelves in the guest room, offer the rest to family, and what we didn't take was donated to the library for the collection or to be sold at the friends of the library store.

All through the grocery, I chatted with people I knew. Several had been to my shop, and others asked me about it. Everyone made a point of saying how glad they were that I was doing so well. You can't go anywhere in Serendipity without running into people who have known you for your whole life, so this wasn't a surprise. What did surprise me was the huge interest in the shop. Mom had said it was because people were so generous and wanted to find a way to help us. I knew part of it was that, but Gran had helped me realize it was partly something else entirely.

One lady in the grocery that day was especially enthusiastic. "Emily, you know the book you gave me when I bought that pair of jeans for my daughter at your shop? Well, when I got home and gave her the bag, she was happy with the jeans because I keep telling her I can't afford designer... She saw the book and threw her arms around me, thanking me over and over. You told me you were putting a book in there as a bonus, but I was so busy that morning I forgot to look. Turns out, that was the next book in a series she has been reading. She wasn't quite done with the previous one yet, but now when she's ready for this one, she's got it. Isn't that funny?"

It was funny, but not as funny as that lady thought. I heard comments like that all the time.

I wanted one of those but thought I should wait....

Mine broke and I needed another.

When I looked into the bag, I wondered if you had somehow read my mind.

All this was super weird, and it was always about the giveaways, never about the items people purchased. A couple of girls came in one day and said they wanted to buy something because maybe whatever I gave them would be important to their life. Like I was foretelling destinies or something. Actually, I think those girls thought I could get them a guy, which was laughable since I didn't have one of my own.

Gran liked a glass of red wine with dinner, and the

grocery store offered a discount if you bought six at once, so I headed for the liquor section. Suddenly, I caught a glimpse of a familiar looking body moving my way. *Adam.* I ducked behind a beer display. He came around the corner concentrating on the contents of the shelves. Without moving or saying anything, I stood there and watched him. Maybe he felt my concentration on him because he suddenly turned my way. Immediately, his frown of concentration turned to surprise, but he quickly masked his features.

"Hey, Emily."

"Adam."

"You look good."

"You mean good as in not dead or good as in pretty?"

"Well. Both, I guess."

"Thanks. It's nice to be alive." I took a couple of steps. "I can even walk on my own. Or did you realize I had to use a walker for a long time and then a cane?" He just stared, but I wasn't going to give him time to respond anyway.

"Hmm. No, I can see that you didn't know that. Lucky you, just being able to forget the old girlfriend and move on with your life." I pulled a bottle off a shelf and set it into the cart. "And hey—thanks a lot for packing up my stuff. My dad found it in the driveway one morning when he left for work. Some of it was still okay even though the boxes all got rained on most of the night, sitting there in a heap on the driveway." I shot him a look. "You have a good day, Adam." I started to push the cart past him, but he grabbed my arm. I held onto the cart and managed not to lose my balance.

"Shut up, Emily, okay? Just shut up." His shaggy hair fell into his face a bit as he looked down at the groceries I'd amassed and back up at me, glowering. "Wine. Flowers. Fancy bread…you're cooking dinner for some guy. That didn't take long. Probably somebody you were seeing when you and me were together." He shook his head as if he was hurt, and my heart started to pound at his accusation.

"You were never satisfied, were you? Always trying to make me into something else. Your new guy will get sick of it, just like I did. I can imagine what kind of patient you were in the hospital and in that rehab place too. Totally self-absorbed and making everybody miserable. Am I right?" He snickered when I didn't reply. "So if you were wondering why I didn't come to visit, it's because I didn't feel like trying to act like I was sorry for you. Everything that's happened, you've brought on yourself." His eyes searched my face. "I see I got your attention with that. Yeah, think about it, Emily. Every wrong job, every breakup, all of it. You brought it on yourself. See you around." He released my arm, pushing it away from him.

How dare he talk to me that way, after what he'd done? All those hours I had hoped Adam would take a few minutes to visit me suddenly rushed into view. He turned on his heel to leave, but I grabbed his jacket, and he stopped, turned, and faced me. This was my chance to let him have it.

"What?" The sneer I'd seen countless times, but behind it was the face of the young man I thought I had loved. I recalled the discussion with Kim about her boyfriend.

"I just—" I took a deep, steadying breath, letting go of my initial defensive reaction. "Adam, the way you ended our relationship was mean and childish." It was classic Adam, but telling him so wouldn't serve any purpose. I was moving past that kind of childish behavior and refused to regress. I stood a little straighter, still holding his gaze. "However, much of what you just said is true."

He stared at me, his eyes registering disbelief. The sneer slipped, and I let go of his jacket.

"I wasted most of my life being self-absorbed, and that fact helped doom our relationship. You're right that I was a rotten patient too. And it turns out, I'm glad you didn't come to visit, *ever*, after I woke up." His eyes drilled into mine, and I turned away from the intensity, put another item in the cart as I spoke. "Believe it or not, you did me a huge favor by dumping me when you did. That's one of the reasons I looked hard at my life and realized it needed to change drastically if it's to be worthwhile at all. I was on a road toward living out my years and having nothing to be proud of, and I can thank you for helping me see that." I chanced another look into his eyes. He was listening, not preparing to bark at me.

"But you're wrong about me seeing anyone else while you and I were together. I would never do that." I pointed down at the cart's contents. "These are my grandmother's groceries, and I'm buying the daisies for myself. I like myself again, after having a long hard fall off the pedestal I used to stand on in my own mind." I held out my hand. "Adam, thank you. I hope you have a good life. I plan to do the same."

His face had totally lost that ugly mask he'd been wearing. Adam smiled wryly and shifted his gaze to my hand for a moment before taking it gently and giving it a quick light squeeze. "I'm glad you're better, Emily. I'm glad you can look at the past differently now." He sighed as he dropped my hand. "And I hope good things come your way."

I took a deep breath, feeling confident. "They will. I'm not sure how, but they will."

Half a minute after Adam left the store, I saw Gran enter. Something made me look into the cart, and I quickly took out the haphazard selection of hard liquor I had added while spilling my guts to Adam. I returned those bottles to the shelves before pushing the cart to meet Gran.

"Emily, you've gotten everything, I see. I hope you weren't waiting too long. I talked with a friend at the drugstore for a while...." She tipped her head, looked into my eyes. "Are you all right, honey?"

"Um. Yeah—yes. Yes, I'm great." And I meant it.

Chapter Nineteen

I typed the text and pressed *Send* before I could change my mind.

Hey. Know anybody who needs his house cleaned?

David had said he would hold the job for me. It wasn't much money but would be helpful to my bank account and effort to get my own place. It might hurt a little if David was back to being "just a friend of the family," but I could handle it if I needed to. My cell phone rang in less than a minute. David's name displayed on the caller ID.

"Hello? That was quick." *Try not to sound desperate or over the top.*

"Hi. I'm at the airport, heading home. You're up to it, you think? The place is basically a wreck."

I laughed. "And this is news?"

"Watch it, Emily. You're not an invalid anymore, so we don't have to take abuse from you." He chuckled. "Okay, it's more of a wreck than you've ever seen it. I definitely need you but let me get home so I can run a frontend loader through once or twice. That way you'll at least be able to find the surfaces that need cleaning." He paused as a loudspeaker in the airport blared. "So what works for you? I get in tonight. How about Saturday?"

"I've learned that business drops to nothing on Saturday afternoon, so I'm closing the shop at noon. Any time after that would work. My busy life is basically an empty planner calendar somebody gave me for Christmas."

His deep chuckle had a surprising effect on my stomach. "That'll change, no doubt. The guys will be calling soon enough, and I'll never get another text from you. Poor old me."

"Yeah. My heart bleeds." Poor old you, the man who has always refused to settle down in a relationship.

"Seriously, girl. Have some respect."

"For my elders? You're right, David. Since you have one foot in the grave and everything, I'll try to be nice." Somehow the usual teasing about age wasn't doing it for me today.

Neither of us said anything for a long minute.

"Are you driving these days, or can I pick you up?"

"Not driving yet." Partly because my car was still not repaired, and I needed money to accomplish that. "If you don't mind picking me up, Gran or Mom or Dad can probably bring me back."

"No need for that. Are you still living at your parents' house in that closet?"

"It's not a closet." I looked around the plain, peaceful space that had been such a haven as I worked through the tumult of my past.

"I've heard a little about your shop. I'll come before noon so I can see what life-changing item you might give me." He chuckled, and I tried to laugh with him.

Casual, casual. "See you tomorrow."

"Great. Be sure to save me something special, Emily."

Considering David and I have known each other for literally my entire life, some of the highlights of which are documented on Gran's wall of fame in the hall by her bathroom, I shouldn't be nervous about seeing him or about going to his house to clean it. I'd done that ever since middle school except for these months since my wreck. I also refused to be nervous about his browsing the items in my shop and wanting me to save him something special. I wasn't sure how I felt about my premonitions about the items I gave away and whether they were predictors of some sort. Still, hearing David's active disbelief was a bit disquieting. I found myself hoping I wouldn't experience an urge to give him something.

Saturday at about fifteen minutes before noon, I saw him pull up to the curb outside my shop. I had changed my shirt three times before leaving home, more reminiscent of pre-date primping than gearing up for house cleaning detail. But hey—I didn't want to look awful.

I told Mom that David was picking me up to go out and clean his house and that I'd check in when I returned. She was glad to know I felt like trying to do that old job again. I'd been helping her some and kept my own space spotless, which was easy since I had fewer and fewer belongings to clean around.

Unfortunately, Mom kept insisting that David was interested in me which kind of forced me to insist he was not. I wanted him to be interested, had wanted that for a lot of years when I was younger, but had finally decided it just wasn't likely to happen. The twisted part was that I'd given up on the possibility long ago, before that kiss by the river. Having that single moment of romance with David and then being flung back to "just friends" status again was infinitely worse than never tasting his lips. At least I think it was worse. And I wouldn't tell anyone about it, because as days and weeks passed, I wondered if that memorable evening had, in fact, truly happened.

I definitely wouldn't tell Mom about it and fuel her fire. As it was, every time I pointed out the ways in which David and I were worlds apart, Mom countered with something about how we had grown up together. In my mind that made it less likely that we would ever end up romantically involved and even a little weird if we did. Would you want to kiss your sister? I hope not, and I really think most of us considered the Standish kids and the Kincaid kids, at a minimum, first cousins, when in reality we were no blood relation at all.

David came through the door of my shop, whistling poorly. "Good morning, Emily." He looked delicious in faded jeans, joggers, a dark knit shirt, and the Carhartt jacket I had worn one evening. "I thought I might see if there's anything I need to buy."

"Hi, David. Um. Sure. Go ahead and browse." I shifted from one foot to the other. "It somehow feels wrong to encourage you to buy anything, because I will just end up dusting it at your house."

"Hmm. Good point." His actions belied his words as he slowly walked along, looking carefully at the items displayed.

I tidied the few things that had been put out of place by other shoppers. I was eager to close up and get into the car with him, head out of town, and see the tree farm again. "Do you think we should stop in today and see Lillian? I'd like to make sure she's still getting along okay with the computer."

"We can do that. I know she'd be glad for a visit." David turned toward me while he was talking but seemed enthralled with his browsing. When it was nearly noon, he took something off the shelf and brought it to me.

"I used to have one of these when I was a kid and have always been sorry I got rid of it. How much, Emily?"

"It's a wind-up alarm clock."

He chuckled. "Yes, I realize that."

"You have a radio alarm clock." I had dusted it enough times to be able to describe it in detail.

"Right."

"But there's nothing wrong with the one you have, is there?"

"Nope. It works fine. This is just a sentimental purchase. Anything wrong with that?"

"No. Not at all." It was one item I hadn't expected to sell, since it was so outdated. David handed the clock to me, and my breath caught as our fingertips touched. That was so stupid—*I* was so stupid—to be affected by him. *Just friends. Just friends.*

I quoted him a price. He laid some bills on the counter, and I wrapped the clock and slipped it into a bag. He watched me carefully, a half-grin on his face.

"Am I going to get one of your famous extras? Word on the street is that you're doing some prognosticating with your giveaways." He looked hopeful yet cynical. I quickly glanced around the room to see if I'd get a feeling to give an item to David.

Shrugging, I fluffed the tissue around the clock and handing the bag to David. "Sometimes I get an idea of what to give someone, and sometimes it doesn't happen. Sorry David, but it seems you're not getting a freebie."

He sighed dramatically. "Just my luck. But I guess I'm getting you for the afternoon, so I shouldn't complain."

Hmm. Don't I wish he meant that a different way? "You're a good sport. Um. Let me hit the bathroom before we leave." When I was returning to the shop area from the storage room where the bathroom was, I felt compelled to open one of the boxes I hadn't looked in yet. Without thinking, I pulled out a framed picture of my favorite boy band from middle school years.

He looked up when I came back. "Here you go, David." I showed him the photo and slid it into the bag.

He watched me, crestfallen. "Is this a joke?"

"Nope. I got a feeling to give you that, so I am. That's the way it works. I get the feeling, and just do it. Nobody can accuse me of malice aforethought, because there's no forethought at all."

"Oh, well." He sounded disappointed, but his facial expression showed he just considered the whole experience entertaining. Even to me, it was a weird item to give him, but I had my usual strong feeling about it and just let it happen.

"Maybe you could change out the photo, so it isn't a total waste. Do you have a picture you've been meaning to frame?"

"Nope. I don't do much of that, as you may recall."

"Well, here's a chance to start. In case there's a special picture." Perhaps of the current out-of-town girlfriend? Not that the frame was anything great. It had probably come from the local dollar store back in the day.

I locked the door and headed to the passenger side of his silver BMW. As I reached for the door handle, his hand was already on it.

"Whoa. Nice. Thank you." Surprised at the display of old-fashioned manners, I slipped into the seat and grinned at him as he gently pushed the door until it latched. When he was in the driver's seat, he turned toward me.

"I'm trying to develop courtly manners. Read about it in a men's magazine somewhere, and I realized Dad had treated Mom that way. Opening doors for her, walking on the street side of a sidewalk. Old-fashioned stuff, but you know what? I think it shows a level of caring that's not evident in a lot of relationships."

I decided to let the word "relationship" slide, since he and I didn't have one. "I don't know about men walking on the street side of a sidewalk. What's that about?"

He shrugged, maneuvering around traffic on the square and pulling onto North Main. "I guess in case a driver loses control of their vehicle and jumps the curb, the man is there to take the brunt of the blow. Or maybe just fend off a loose hubcap." He laughed at himself. "Anyway if you notice me doing that, it's an effort at courtly manners. I've not suddenly gone crazy."

I watched him as he talked. He seemed somehow different today.

"You're very cheery."

He looked over at me briefly. "Yes, I am. Why wouldn't I be? I'm driving down the road with the prettiest woman in Serendipity, after all."

My heart skipped, and I told it not to get excited. "Kind words and I thank you."

"Not kind. Just truthful." We passed a billboard for one of the local chain restaurants in town. "Hey—I didn't ask about lunch. We could go back."

"I ate a sandwich just before you arrived, but thanks. If I'd known you were going to offer, I would have saved my appetite." I rubbed my leg which was less swollen and less painful each day. I was glad to have graduated out of stretchy yoga pants and back into my jeans.

"Maybe we can get something later. I bet you'll work up a big appetite shoveling out my mess." He winced as he said it. "It really is bad. I wasn't kidding about that, Emily."

"I'm a pro, remember? Plus, I have a backup plan. If it's too horrible, I will suddenly develop a relapse and have to be taken to my parents' house immediately."

"Ah. Impressive plan. Since I'm on this courtly manners jag, I'd probably fall for it too." He was silent a moment, considering his next words. "I notice you didn't refer to it as 'home.' Is that significant?"

"Sort of, I guess. I'm really looking forward to having my own place. Right now, it's financially impossible, but I'm making more money at the shop than I expected and I'm saving every penny. Mom and Dad have been awesome to fix up that little room and let me do pretty much whatever I want. But before long, I'll have to get my own place."

"Have to?" He frowned. "I imagine everyone is happy to have you there."

"Everyone is being kind. Even Taylor and Hannah. I probably can't explain it very well, but it's just time for me to move on. I have spent all my life getting nowhere."

"So you're getting rid of the past one paper sack at a time?"

Was he poking fun at me? "Hmm. Yes, I guess so."

"Seems some of the possessions you're getting rid of are doing some real good in other people's lives." He paused, shaking his head in surprise.

"It does seem that way," I agreed. "It makes me happy to be helping people. I can't say I've done a lot of that in the past."

He glanced at me and winked. "You don't give yourself much credit, do you, Emily?"

"I think I know my own history. I can't change the past, but I can sure do my best from here on out."

"And getting your own place is next on the agenda?"

I shrugged. "Dunno. I hope so. When the shelves are emptied for the last time, that's when I can move on." I turned toward him, deciding to go ahead and say what was in my heart. "Okay, you're going to think I'm completely nuts, but it feels like I can't move into my future until I let go of some pieces of the past."

He was quiet, letting that sink in. "I don't think you're nuts. I think you've given this a lot of consideration, and I respect that. But—are you saying you want to get rid of *everything*?"

"Well, I have some stuff at the house that I'm keeping. Clothes, a few books, a couple of picture albums and scrapbooks. Plus some keepsakes I can't seem to part with no matter how many times I try to set them out on the shelves for customers."

"Radical minimalism."

"I guess." I looked out my side window at the

scenery that used to be so familiar but which I was able to see with new eyes after being away for months. I had always considered it boring, yet our county was lovely. Now we were in sight of the tree farm and, as usual, my heart started to beat a little faster. David turned into the driveway and pulled up to Lillian's house. When he opened the door for me—this cavalier stuff took longer than just getting out on my own, believe it or not—we went up to the front door. I took the steps a little more easily and quickly than I had last time when Gran and I were here. David knocked loudly twice, opened the door, and had me go in first.

Matthew Singer flew toward me from the kitchen. "Em'ly! You comed to visit Miss Lillian and me!"

I sat in a nearby chair and pulled him into a tight, if somewhat chocolatey, hug. "Hey, Matthew. It's great to see you. I guess you're helping Miss Lillian bake cookies?"

"Yes. And they are yummy!"

Lillian walked in, wiping her hands on an apron. "Emily, for a girl who says she doesn't want cookies, you have arrived at the wrong time. We have a couple dozen cooling and another dozen baking right now." She looked lovingly down at Matthew. "Honey, you want to bring a plateful in here and some napkins?" He immediately raced back to the kitchen.

"Oh my. And to think my intentions were completely honorable." I patted my thighs. "At least, I'll burn a few calories today. My first time cleaning David's house since the wreck."

Lillian sighed. "You'd better take a few cookies with you to keep your strength up, dear. I'm afraid David has been a slob his entire life."

David dropped onto the couch. "Wow, Mom. That's not necessary, is it?"

She shot him a good-natured look. "The cookies or the brutal honesty?"

"The honesty. Cookies are always necessary."

Matthew walked carefully into the room carrying a porcelain plate piled with cookies. He also had some crumpled napkins in his hand. Each of us took a cookie, and after he set the plate down, he handed the napkins around.

"Miss Lillian bakes the best cookies," he announced.

"Even better when I have a good helper." Lillian bit into one and winked at Matthew.

"I thought I'd stop in on the way to my other job to see if you need any tech support with the computer, Lillian."

Matthew sat in the little rocker that was just his size and took a huge bite of cookie. "Miss Lillian wants the 'puter in her office."

"Oh?" David and I both said.

Lillian sank into a chair and smoothed a napkin on her knee. "Well. Yes, I think I do want to put it in—the office." She straightened a bit. "I've given it some thought, and Matthew and I have discussed it. We think Harry would be okay with me having it in there...."

"And we need to make the office pretty 'cuz Miss Lillian's a girl," Matthew added. "Grandpa Harry isn't using it now. He wants Miss Lillian to be happy."

Grandpa Harry? Matthew hadn't moved here until after Harry died, besides being no relation to the Standish family at all. Still, it was cute coming from Matthew, and Lillian obviously didn't mind.

David nodded. "Dad's—" He cleared his throat to start over. "The office does have kind of a macho theme. How can I help, Mom?"

She reached out and took his hand. "Everything is such a step, isn't it? Thank you, honey. When I have a better idea what I want, I'll let you know how to help." She squeezed his hand briefly, released it, and leaned back again. "Little by little, we are finding our way to a new life. Not a life we would have chosen, but we'll make the most of what we have, I know."

An image of the unforgettable Kimberly Rose sprang to my mind.

Lillian looked at Matthew, who was beaming at her. "And some of the surprises in the new part of our lives have been wonderful."

I promised to come help in whatever way I could with the office changeover, including setting up the computer in its new habitat. Not long after that, we said good-bye to Lillian and Matthew.

David helped me into the car again. I waited until he started the car before speaking. "Your mom is great, David. She's a really strong lady."

He nodded. "I agree on both counts. Surprises me about the office, but I think it's a good decision. We all still miss Dad, but the pain is less raw than it was. I think he's proud of how we've been able to keep the farm going and take care of Mom. Take care of each other, for that matter."

I watched the trees out my side window as we drove up the track toward his plot of ground. "Did you say you're going to put cabins on the farm this spring?"

"That's right. The first two are being set next week." He rubbed his hand over his sexy day-old beard growth. "I wasn't sure about it when Melissa first brought up the idea, but I've done a little research. It seems like a solid plan. I hope the B&B part won't be more than Mom wants to do. She keeps pretty busy most of the time already. She's always going to a meeting or volunteering somewhere."

"That does seem like a lot of work if Lillian's doing all of it. Cleaning and changing linens and all."

He nodded. "And serving breakfast each morning. We know we'll probably have to hire part-time help, but so far she hasn't wanted to put an ad in the paper. It's her call, of course, and she has held firm on not advertising a job opening yet."

"Hmm. Surely, she'll put an ad in the paper soon so you can get started renting the cabins."

We rounded the last curve, and David's house came into view. I took a deep—and I hope silent—breath. I had always admired how well the long, ranch-style house suited its setting with its patios front and back topped by shallow-sloped roofs. It was as different from the other houses on the farm as David was from the other family members. Lillian lived in the original big white farm house. Carla's was a small bungalow in the Craftsman style, and Jim had a two-story log cabin. Of course, they weren't side by side to compare. They were separated by acres of Christmas trees.

"Home sweet home." David pushed the garage

door opener. One aspect that was new about today—I had never before pulled into the garage of David's home. It was cozy when the door slid down enclosing us in an intimate silence. The moment was brief, as he quickly got out and opened my car door for me. With a dramatic groan, he flung open the door that led from the garage into the house.

Wow. He had been only partly kidding about the condition of his home.

I preceded him into the kitchen area and glanced hesitantly toward the living room. "David. Seriously. Do you even have one clean glass in the place?"

"Of course. I bought some the other day. Problem solved." He looked at me sheepishly and started to pick up random items, look at them, and either put them somewhere reasonable, such as dirty glasses in the sink, or unreasonable, such as old newspapers back on the couch cushion where they'd been a minute ago.

"I need a drink," I said, slumping onto a stool at the bar that was covered in six inches of mail.

He shook his head. "No drinking on the job." He walked toward to the fridge, but I was afraid of what might be inside it. "What'll you have?"

I held up a hand to stop him from opening the door. "Coffee?"

"Yes. I have it covered." He reached for a plastic grocery bag and pulled out a box of instant-brew pods. The coffeemaker water reservoir was empty, but it still took just a couple of minutes to fill it and get my coffee in process. He opened a cabinet, and there were, in fact, no clean coffee cups. I sighed and took a couple of dirty ones out of the sink, washed, and dried them. After a deep drink of the elixir of life, I sucked in a breath.

"I was in a terrible accident, David, and I feel a relapse coming on."

He started, recovered, and grinned again. "No fair going the sympathy route. You can see I need help here."

"You need... Oh, okay." I gulped more coffee. "Make me another cup of this and leave me alone for three hours. When you come back, either the place will look better or I'll have died trying."

He paled. "Don't even joke about that. Please."

"I'm serious—about the coffee and the three hours, anyway."

"I could go outside and do something useful, I guess. Jim always has a list of projects for me." He took a scrawled note off the fridge, folded it, and slid it into a back pocket of his jeans.

"Okay, that's your call." I started rummaging in the

sink cabinet where I used to keep the cleaning supplies. There was disastrous clutter even in this area which surely hadn't been disturbed in a very long time. I knelt on the floor and started pulling everything out of the cabinet.

"What are you doing? Don't worry about what's not even visible, Emily."

I glared at him. "I'm the cleaning professional, remember."

He put up his hands and stepped back. "Okay. I'll be outside. Call if you need me."

"Chicken!"

He started making cackling sounds as he switched jackets and boots, and I couldn't help laughing. I had been taking care of his house for years, and it was both painful to see it in such an awful state and encouraging that he needed my help. I pulled off some paper towels and started cleaning the inside of the cabinet, remembering how this strange symbiosis had begun.

***

The door opened after I knocked on it a few times. I wasn't going away until David Standish answered. I was a woman on a mission. Waiting, I looked back at the scenery. He sure had a great view from up here on the hill. Evergreen trees and occasional glades of grass seemed to go on forever. If I stood on tiptoe, I could see the edge of the lake too. Wow, he was lucky to have such an awesome place. I turned back toward the house when I heard footfalls coming near. He flung the door open. His dark hair, businessman short, was tousled, and there were pillow marks on his face. When he recognized me, his expression went from angry to just perturbed, as if being bugged by a bothersome kid sister. I had seen this expression on his face before and had probably worn it loads of times in my own home, burdened as I was with three younger siblings.

"Emily. This is a surprise. What brings you way out here?" He looked around for a car but saw my bicycle on its kickstand at the edge of the walk near the driveway. "You rode your bike? Pretty ambitious."

"It's not that far. Plus I'm in good shape." I could have asked Mom or Dad to drive me, but Dad had to work and Mom was really tied down with my rambunctious twin sisters.

"I guess you must be. Not sure I could manage to ride a bike from your house to mine."

"Well, you're older."

He groaned. "I'm not on Social Security yet. I'm only twenty-four." He released his hold on the door and took a step back. "Come on in. Let me get you something to drink." He padded barefoot across the wide, hardwood boards of the open-plan room to the kitchen area. He was wearing a rumpled T-shirt and jeans that looked as if he'd pulled them out of the hamper.

I followed him, looking around at the classy, but very messy, room. "I'm just fourteen. I hate being a kid. I can't wait to grow up and get my own place."

"Oh, sure. I said the same thing at your age. Every kid thinks that. But try not to waste your energy wishing you were at a different stage of your life. Make the most of where you are now. I know you don't want to hear it, but you're at a great age, Emily. You'll make lots of memories with your friends that you'll look back on for the rest of your life."

"I don't make memories, David. I go to school, do homework, help Mom around the house."

He set a can of Coke in front of me at the bar that separated the kitchen area from the living area. "Please don't expect me to feel sorry for you. I'm out of college, have a job, and work all the time. I've helped here on the tree farm my entire life, so when I come home on the weekends Dad has my weekend planned out for me. I get home Friday from traveling all week for my job, work here all weekend, and early Monday, I'm at the airport getting ready to take off again."

"But you get to see the world all week."

"I get to see the inside of airports and airplanes and taxis and business office buildings. Sometimes it's cool, like when I hit it off with…somebody at a client's office and we go out for a drink or dinner. So there are perks. I like it." He shrugged and grinned. "I love it, really, but you've caught me at the end of a very long week."

I popped the top of the Coke and took a sip. "You have such a great house."

"Yep." He spooned aromatic grounds into a filter, poured water in the top of the coffeemaker, and walked over to sit on the stool next to me. "It's just the way I envisioned it. That's important in life, if you're looking for tips. Envision goals and set out to make them come true."

"Funny you would say that, David." I took a big swig of Coke to help muster courage. "Because I am envisioning myself going to Disneyworld with the church youth group."

"Cool. Hope that works out for you."

"I have to earn the money to go."

"Really? Very good. What are you doing to earn it?"

I pulled the brochures out of the back pocket of my shorts. It took me a minute to get them unfolded. I smoothed them with my hands onto the counter. "I'm selling this quality merchandise. You can subscribe to magazines or buy candles or wrapping paper." I carefully read the headline aloud from the top of the last brochure. "Or other 'home décor items.'"

"No thanks."

"What?" I'd ridden how many miles of hills to get out here, only to be turned down by somebody who had just lectured me about making memories?

"I said no thanks. I don't need any of that stuff." He walked over to the coffeemaker which had produced a pot full of dark aromatic liquid that I knew would taste horrible. David opened a cabinet door and took down a mug, leaving the interior of the cabinet now empty. As he poured the coffee, I took a better look at his kitchen area. The sink was full of mugs, bowls, and spoons. A pan on the stovetop had what looked like cold, hardened chili drooled down the side. A couple of pizza boxes had been tossed on the other counter. David Standish, successful businessman and all around hunk, was a slob.

"How am I going to make memories if I don't get to go anywhere? And how can I get what I'm envisioning if people don't buy this fundraiser stuff?" *Answer me that, smart guy.*

He took a long draw on the hot coffee. "Get a job.

Do something that's worth money to people, and you'll earn it instead of guilting people into buying stuff to clutter up their space."

"Some of these items would make great Christmas gifts for family and friends on your shopping list," I recited from the training session our youth minister had presented.

"Emily, forget it. Nobody gave me what I have, and I think it's important for kids to learn to work for what they get. That's the real world."

David had money. I could tell that from how nice his house was—not huge, but it was class all the way.

I leaned back and crossed my arms. "Okay. You're the expert. How did you get the money for this house?"

"Worked almost every day of my life on a Christmas tree farm. Plus, my dad and brother and I did a lot of the work of building the house with some help here and there from a plumber or electrician friend. And, of course, a stone mason."

He sat down next to me again and sighed. "I tell you what. You clean my house, and I'll give you cash. Put that in your fund for the trip."

It felt like a staring contest for a minute. I kept thinking he would cave and buy something from the catalog, but what sense did that make when I could earn lots more from cleaning the house? I'd been trained by the best. My mom and Grandma Reba didn't let a dust bunny survive overnight in their homes.

"Okay. I'll do it."

David let out a big breath. "Great. I gotta tell you, I'm relieved. Those big brown eyes of yours are the best sales tools I've run up against in a long time. You need to work on a better pathetic look, though, if you're going to sell this stuff." He nudged the brochures toward me, and I re-folded them and shoved them back into my pocket.

"I'm not pathetic, so I won't be developing a pathetic look."

"Good for you, Emily. Now let's look at this project you've signed on for...."

I had worked hard that day to get David's house in decent shape. Typical bachelor, I guess, he used everything in his cupboards before washing a single dish. He eventually bought a dishwasher and either didn't load it or left clean dishes sitting in it until I arrived and emptied it. After the first couple of Saturdays, when I had piles to wade through, I went in every Thursday after school or after whatever day job I had and did maintenance cleaning. Twice a year, I deep cleaned and he paid extra for that. I left him a bill at the end of every month, handwritten on notebook paper in the early days, and he mailed me a check. He mailed the checks from wherever he was traveling that week, because he knew I would enjoy looking at the postmarks and stamps.

I had kept that little job for years, from the age of fourteen until I was twenty-five and had the wreck. There was a lot of *déjà* vu in standing here looking at a disaster so similar to the other. Was I making any progress toward a new life, or was I locked in some kind of infinite loop?

***

My first day back at David's house was good but weird. I liked that he didn't treat me as if I was in danger of breaking at any moment. Obviously, he hadn't made a big effort to pre-clean. Heck, the joke he'd made previously about needing to run a front end loader through the place wasn't so far off. Since coming back to Serendipity from rehab, I had been getting rid of stuff, and here was David, evidently sitting on the mother lode of pizza boxes, maybe not cleaned out since my accident. Some things don't change. I couldn't help humming as I worked, because it was great to be needed.

David came in through the garage door looking pleased. "Hey. Are you done? It looks like home again."

I pushed the vacuum into the closet and closed the door, faced him with my hands on my hips.

"Never do that again."

"What? Ask if you're done?"

"Ha. Never ever let your home get so trashed. There's no reason for it, David."

He grinned. "Man, Emily, I didn't expect a lecture."

"I think it's time you got one. Years ago when I came here expecting you to buy a few cheap trinkets to help me go on a youth group trip, you lectured me about working for my money. You know what? That made total sense, and I've benefited from being willing to work instead of taking shortcuts. But here's your lecture. You have a time-consuming job. I get that. You also have a home that's worth taking care of. That includes washing dishes, taking the recycling to the pick-up station, and putting your trash out at the road once a week. I give you credit for not expecting your mom to do it for you, but you're a big boy, David. You don't need me to do basic stuff like that. You have a couple of hours in a weekend to do something that simple. You were to the point of a health concern in that kitchen."

He began to chuckle, and I got wound up.

I stomped my foot. "Now, stop it. You take me seriously."

He covered his face with both hands for a second, and when he removed them his demeanor was completely solemn. "Emily, you're right. You're one hundred percent correct. Maybe not about a health concern in the kitchen—okay, maybe even that. I'm not laughing at you. I was just struck by how lucky we both are that you're here feeling energetic enough to clean up my mess and to give me grief for creating it in the first place." He gave me a quick, side-arm hug. "You're a miracle, Emily. To all of us. Now, let's eat. I'm starving. Should I order pizza?"

I punched him on the arm, because I knew he'd just said it because he'd amassed a mountain of pizza boxes in my absence.

"Much as I love pizza or, at least, did until I walked in here today, if you're offering to buy a meal, I'd like to go somewhere and sit down."

"Seriously?" He gestured to the sparkling clean bar. "We can sit down here. It's great."

"Take me out for non-fast food, or I will write a letter to the editor detailing the disaster this house was in when I arrived. You don't want that on your permanent record."

"No kidding. I don't need advertising in the paper, indicating I'm in need of a housekeeper. It's hard enough to be a bachelor around here without that extra stress." He walked into the kitchen, and one by one opened sparkling cabinet doors that were now full of clean dishes. "What restaurant can I tempt you with, Emily? Nothing is too good for the woman who holds my reputation in her hands."

I really did hold his reputation in my hands, but not for the reason he was alluding to. When you clean every inch of a man's house, you learn about him, whether or not you see him face-to-face on a regular basis. Photos, movie and theater tickets, parking stubs, receipts.... Oh, the receipts. David was a generous gift giver, and there were many beneficiaries of his generosity all over the country down through the years. Oh yeah, I could tell stories. But I wouldn't, because I genuinely cared for David.

He snapped his fingers. "There's a new place in Mendacious. I hear it has great steaks and seafood. How does that sound?"

I looked down at my grimy clothes. "Good, but actually, maybe another time." I need some detoxing before I could go out among people." I sighed. "You can just take me back to Mom and Dad's." Feeling a bit like Cinderella, I couldn't keep the self-pity out of my voice.

He looked disappointed. "How about this? I'll hook up with Jim after I drop you off and let him work me until I reach the breaking point—it's our macho brother-bonding time. I'll shower and pick you up for a late dinner. Would that work?"

I stood staring at him for too long. That sounded like a date. Nah—not possible. "Um. Okay. That sounds really good. But don't think dinner out pays me for the magic I performed here today."

He looked at the spotless bar top again, walked into the kitchen area, and examined the countertops.

"You didn't leave me a bill, Emily Kincaid."

I laughed. "Wow. I *am* out of practice."

"I save them," he said, pulling a small notepad and a pen out of the junk drawer and handing them to me.

"I can believe it. One of these days when I least expect it, there'll be a mountain of my bills wadded up in the middle of the living room."

"Maybe. Or maybe I put them into an album each time and store them in a locked safe because I'm just that sentimental."

"Um. Yeah, I don't think so, but just in case, I'll work on my handwriting." I took a little extra time in writing out the bill, adding a flourish to the "y" at the end of my name. "Okay. Ready to go."

David picked up the paper and shook his head. "No way."

"Huh? Hey—it was a lot more work than usual, in spite of only doing some basic cleaning in three rooms so far. Next weekend I'll start in the others. Do *not* trash the kitchen in the meantime." I sighed. "I know I'm slower than in the old days, but David, this place was a total wreck."

He pulled out a money clip and peeled bills off the outside, making the total much more than I had requested.

"Not a penny more—or less." Stone-faced, he returned the money clip to his pocket and took my jacket out of the coat closet, and handed it to me. "I'm so glad you're better, Emily. Even my house is happy about that."

He put on his jacket and drove me back to my parents'. We didn't say much, but it was okay to have some silence. I was lost in my thoughts, and maybe he was too. If I could get back to doing this job each week, I'd be even closer to becoming independent, even if it was a *squeaking by* kind of independence. Cleaning was great exercise, and I was already feeling a pleasant soreness in muscles I hadn't worked as much as I should. I'd have to get someone to drive me, if I planned to resume my Thursday afternoon routine. If I fixed my beat-up car before I found a new place, my move would be much further in the future.

He pulled up at the back door of my parents' house and shut off the engine. "Seven o'clock, okay?"

"Yes," I said. "I'll be ready."

After my shower, I carefully straightened my hair so it wouldn't have its persistent obnoxious wave on one side. I treated myself to some reading time, propped up on my bed with cushions at my back. I don't know how long I read, but when Mom knocked at my door, I was sound asleep. After making sure I had plenty of time, I joined her in the kitchen for a cup of tea.

She poured the hot water into her favorite teapot and carried it to the table, paused for a good look at me. "Sweetie, did I wake you from a nap? I'm so sorry."

I yawned, unable to keep from it. "Yes, I fell asleep after I got back from cleaning at David's house. It was a terrible mess, Mom. I don't think he'd picked up a single piece of litter since the last time I cleaned. It's not great now, but at least it's habitable. *Men*." I tried not to grin saying it, because the coming dinner with David seemed to put us on a different footing than in the past.

She nodded. "Yes indeed. They're a dependent bunch."

"Um. Mom? I'll be out this evening. Leaving around seven." I cleared my throat. "Not sure what time I'll get home."

Concern flashed across her features. "Oh? Going out with friends, sweetie?"

Poor Mom—I hadn't been out much since my wreck. "Kind of. Yes. David and I are going to a new steakhouse in Mendacious. He said it was good. Maybe you've heard about it."

Visibly relaxing, she took the bags out of the teapot, set them aside, and poured the amber liquid into each delicate cup.

"Dinner with David. That's news."

"It's not a big deal. He has to eat. I have to eat. We haven't seen each other much in a while…you know."

She sipped her tea and smiled. "Hmm. I thought something like this would happen soon."

"Mom. Please. It's just dinner. We're friends. Practically related."

"Not related at all, and I think it's wonderful. Your dad will be pleased too."

"You're trying to make this into something it's not."

Suppressed laughter crinkled her eyes. "One of us is, Emily. You two have fun. I won't worry if you're with David."

***

The twenty-minute drive to Mendacious was a weird kind of trip. David had arrived to pick me up at a couple of minutes before seven, and before he could knock on my door, I opened it.

"Hey. You're prompt," he said looking surprised.

"Sure. Free food—don't want to miss that opportunity." I felt a blush coming on, remembering Mom's reaction earlier when I'd told her about tonight's dinner. I kept my face averted while locking the door and walking to the car so David didn't notice my pink cheeks.

"Something wrong?" He opened the car door for me and stood so close I couldn't politely look away.

"No. Nothing at all. Why?" I slipped into the seat, and he closed the door and rounded the vehicle. He slid in behind the wheel. "Your face is red. Did you get windburn rushing around cleaning my house, or are you embarrassed?"

"Sometimes I hate having such pale skin. And, okay, it's not windburn."

"Your skin is beautiful." He started the vehicle and backed out. "So why are you embarrassed?"

I felt my face grow warmer at his compliment. "Oh, Mom. I told her who I was going out with—well, not that I was going out, just dinner—and you know how she is. Kind of a romantic."

"Is she? Well, I guess that's one of the best parts about living alone. You don't have to check in with anybody when you go somewhere, and you don't have to tiptoe in when you come back home."

"I bet."

"I'll be glad to help you find something, if you want. Whenever you're ready. I understand you still have things to redistribute before you can move."

"Thanks. That's a nice offer. It probably needs to be something centrally located so I can walk wherever I need to go. It may be a while before I can afford to get my car repaired."

"You're certain that a new place is more important than getting your wheels back?"

"Yep. I've never lived on my own, and it's time." I felt it more strongly each day.

"Oh. I guess I thought you had been on your own before. Where did you live when the wreck happened?"

I stared out the side window at the dark scenery.

"Sorry. Didn't hear you. Where?"

"I lived with my boyfriend. Adam."

"Who is now where?"

"He's around. He has a new girlfriend."

"Oh. You okay with all that?"

"Yes. As it happens, Adam and I have made peace. It's one more matter I had to take care of before I could move on with my life." I stopped, not knowing where that statement had come from or that I'd felt that way about Adam.

"Really?"

"Um…yes."

"Well, good for you. Sounds like you've got everything figured out."

I looked out the side window again. "Does it? I can't say it feels that way."

We were in Mendacious, and he had pulled into a parking space in a brightly lit parking lot with a giant sign announcing *Mendacious Steaks*. After David turned off the ignition, he held the keys in his hand and turned to me, his face serious. "There's something different about you since you came back, Emily. Has anyone else mentioned that?"

"No, not that I can think of."

"Well, there is. Since you came back, there is something about you that's just—okay, no. I'm not going to say it." He slid out, shaking his head, and came over to open my door.

"What? What were you going to say? There's something about me that's just—*tall*?" I grinned up at him, but he wasn't playing along. Feeling suddenly brave, I took a half step closer. "Sexy? Irresistible?"

"Good grief, Emily. You were all of the above already, except tall, of course. Don't hold your breath there, since traction after the wreck didn't do it for you. I'm talking about something else entirely."

He walked toward the restaurant, and I stood there in shock for a moment. David thought I was sexy and irresistible? He was at the restaurant door, holding it open. Well, if that was what he thought, he sure had a strange way of showing it.

The place was as nice as David had heard, and besides having a delicious meal, it was a treat to spend a different type of time with him. It seemed we could talk about anything together. On a different footing in this setting, we related to each other simply as two adults. I don't know if it was intentional on his part, but we never once discussed my family or his.

When our plates were cleared, and we lingered at the table, he took another sip of wine and leaned both elbows on the linen tablecloth. "Tell me more about your plans for the future, Emily."

Busted. I hadn't made specific plans—not even mentally—beyond getting my own place. David seemed genuinely interested, and I hated to admit how little visualizing I'd done. He had told me all those years ago of the importance of visualizing what I wanted out of life.

"Um. You know, it's hard to say exactly what my plans are." My eyes flicked around the restaurant to the other diners, some laughing together, others huddled in somber conversation. Probably each of them knew what they wanted out of life and how they would get it. I thought I was changing my life, but now I wondered when I'd really see a difference.

I leaned toward David, lowered my voice. "I could have died in that wreck. The fact that I didn't matters more to me than I could have imagined. Whatever time I have left—if it's minutes, days or years—I'm going to spend it making a difference. I just haven't figured out yet how to do that."

He locked eyes with mine. "You'll discover the right way to make a difference, Emily. I have no doubt of that."

I nodded silently. It was the kind of generally encouraging statement any big brother might have made.

Chapter Twenty

One afternoon I was super surprised to see both Carla Standish and her sister Francie at the door of my shop. When they came in, Francie immediately swept me into a hug.

"Oh, honey, I've been keeping tabs on you from a distance. I'm sorry I didn't get down to see you at the rehab place. Once everyone decided Mom was ready to be on her own, I threw my stuff into a bag and went back to Florida. I had started to feel guilty about being away from Brad and Joseph for such a long time, yet I knew it was important to be here for Mom." She took a step back, holding me by both upper arms. "You look wonderful. You've sure grown up to be a beautiful young woman." She looked at Carla. "Remember what a pretty baby she was?"

"Yes. Pretty, but such a mama's girl." Carla

winked at me. "You'd never let Francie and me hold you, and we were heartbroken. You looked like a baby doll, and we wanted to cuddle you. Back in those days, our families were together so much."

I nodded. "I have some memories of those times, when I was maybe kindergarten age or so. I always felt special when you older kids paid attention to me."

Francie sighed. "I feel bad that my son won't have memories like that. He's our only child, you know, and we don't come back here often to visit. Not as often as I'd like." She looked away, but not before I saw the strain in her eyes. She forced a smile and walked to the other side of the room, her back to us. "I wanted to be sure and shop in the newest store in town while I'm here. *Emily's Dreams* has quite a reputation, I hear, for having exactly the item one needs." She turned to me. "I wonder what that will be for me."

"That part's not guaranteed, I'm sorry to say. Don't think me too weird if I tell you I just give people whatever I'm compelled to give them. I couldn't explain it if I had to."

"Carla showed me the pretty ring holder you gave her."

I shrugged. "I made it in middle school. Got lucky with that particular art class project."

"You know she has it in an étagère in her living room, just in case the right ring comes along."

"Um. No, I didn't."

Carla grinned, coloring a bit. "It's too special to stick away in the bedroom. In fact, it's a perfect match to my living room carpet."

Francie nudged her. "Emily, I think my sister believes what some people in town are saying—that the items you give people are somehow preparing them for a new chapter of their lives. Mom says that's true too. Anyway, I look forward to learning what happens with that ring holder." She winked at her sister. "Now, what shall I buy? It has to fit into my carry-on bag and can't be too heavy." She picked up a pack of note cards. "These are darling. Did you make them?"

"Oh, heck no. I bought those at a charity craft sale." I took the pack of note cards which were heavy white with a circular black tatted pendant on each. "I never can think of anything special enough to write on them. They're so pretty that to me they're intimidating." I slipped the little pack of note cards into a bag before she could say she didn't want them. "But perfect for you."

"They're wonderful, and I agree special occasions will be required in order to use them." Francie unzipped the slim wallet she'd carried on her wrist and handed me a ridiculously large bill. "Take it, Emily. I want you to have it."

"But—Francie—this is just too much."

She zipped the wallet closed. "It's important for me to give you that. It's important for me to help you get your new start. You're part of the family, honey, and I wasn't around to do anything to help while you were hurt."

She sighed with relief when I stopped trying to give the money back to her. I put it into my cash box and crumpled some tissue into her bag to cheer it up since it was nearly empty. Almost of its own volition, my hand reached to the shelf where I had dumped a bunch of magazines I couldn't quite part with yet. The top one was an issue of *People* I had never gotten around to reading.

"Um…Francie?" I held it out to her. She looked at the magazine and laughed.

"Is this my future, Emily? Am I going to become famous—or infamous—enough to be on a magazine cover?"

I shrugged. "I dunno, Francie. It's yours if you want it. I don't have an explanation. I never do."

She slid it into the bag and hugged me. "You're one of a kind, Emily Kincaid. And we all love you."

Carla picked up her big leather handbag. "Well, we need to get back pretty soon. Mom has decided to redo Dad's office while she has additional free labor available."

"Oh. She mentioned it as a possibility last time I was there."

"Yep, she's got that computer now and decided it was time to move it into the office. We all agree Dad wouldn't mind. Believe it or not, we had a family discussion about that, including Melissa and Matthew. Anyway, today's the day we start on it. Can't say I'm looking forward to that."

Francie shook her head, her eyes misting.

"I'm sorry," I said. "I'm sure it's very hard for everyone."

"I'm worried about Mom again," Francie said. "She's done great—really great. But she's insisting she doesn't need help with the B&B, and I'm afraid it's going to be way too much for her. The idea of the bed and breakfast wasn't to work Mom into the ground, but that may be what happens."

Carla set her handbag down again and put her arm around her sister's shoulders. "Honey, don't put this on yourself. You have a life. You and Brad. We've got this. And Mom's realistic, most of the time. She's just being a little bit headstrong on this one matter." She chuckled when Francie shot her a look. "Okay, a lot headstrong."

"Can I help somehow? Lillian has done so much for me. I'd love to have a way to pay her back."

Carla and Francie exchanged looks, and their eyes lit, an idea seeming to occur to both of them simultaneously. Carla put her arm around my shoulders too. "Emily, I think you may be an answer to our prayers. No pressure, of course." We all laughed, but I wasn't sure what we were laughing about.

"You've been wanting a place of your own, right?"

I nodded.

"And you have almost nothing to move into that place."

"Right."

"And you've been helping Mom with her computer."

"Yes…"

"What do you think about moving into one of the tiny cabins and working with Mom on the B&B? There would be breakfast to cook each morning, linens to change when people check out, cleaning, and if she isn't around, greeting guests when they arrive, giving them their keys and a map to the cabin they'll be in."

"Well…"

"You wouldn't need a car," Francie said. "I mean, I understand yours hasn't been repaired yet. Everything is so close, you can walk or use one of the ATVs or pickup trucks. The ATVs are fun, let me tell you."

Carla nodded. "Free rent, and we'll work out the wage. Something fair. We don't want to take advantage."

"No, but we also want someone who's responsible," Francie said. "Having you there would be amazing, because you're practically family."

Even though their brainstorming had me feeling as if I were in the middle of a tennis match, I had to admit it seemed perfect. Yet I wondered about the proximity to David. Since our dinner when I basically dumped my soul on the table as dessert, I'd only heard from him once. Sure, he was back on the road for work and that could entail lots of hours, but that didn't mean he couldn't give me the occasional thought and maybe a quick call, did it? Perhaps he was so good at compartmentalizing the different parts of his life he didn't think of me when I wasn't around. Maybe living on the Christmas tree farm would help clarify what kind of relationship David and I had. I needed to know, because I wasn't going to waste time wanting something I couldn't have. As Kim and I had discussed, I was learning that I was a complete person and didn't require an "other half."

Perhaps the time was coming for me to let go of my years-old crush on David Standish. As Francie had said, they considered me practically family. Maybe he did, too.

Chapter Twenty-One

Mom picked me up as usual the last day my shop was open. "Oh, sweetie," she said quietly as she backed out of the parking space. "It's hard to believe everything is gone. There was so much...."

"There sure was." I sighed, leaning back into the seat. "Aunt Darlene was really nice to let me use that building. I need to get the key back to her soon."

Mom turned the van into traffic and exited the square. "Yes, she was. I'm so glad it worked out. But about the key—she called me today."

"Oh?" That wasn't something that happened often. Aunt Darlene was busy being a businesswoman and mother to perfect progeny.

"Yes. It was a nice surprise. She asked me if I would want to run a consignment shop there, since your little store was so well received. Emily, I've thought about it constantly since talking to her. I think I'll do it." Mom looked delighted at the prospect. I couldn't think when I'd seen her so happy. "I wanted to talk to you before I speak with your father. Darlene asked if we could continue to use the same name for the shop. She wants to register it with the State and go through all the proper channels." She paused at a stop sign on High Street and looked at me. "I wasn't sure what you would think about that. Darlene thinks she might open similar stores in other small towns around that don't have much shopping available. Bit by bit, with Serendipity being the test case. And she said she would pay you something each year for using the name and logo you came up with."

"Really?" I was in shock. My simple little idea might have a future?

"I told her she should call you, but she insisted she needed to know whether I wanted to run it first of all. She said she's a stickler for having personnel who are competent. I found that flattering, coming from Darlene."

"Yeah. No kidding. I'm glad you're interested, Mom. I think it's a great idea."

"When you first mentioned opening a shop, I wasn't sure about the idea, but it really has been a wonderful addition to Serendipity. Now, we'll take consignments, so people can earn some spending money or buy things inexpensively. I imagine the days of the surprising freebies are gone though."

"I guess you can't give other people's stuff away for free, like I could."

"Exactly. Well, if you agree, I'll speak to your father tonight. I think he's been concerned I'll be at loose ends once you and the twins are gone."

He wasn't the only one who was concerned about that.

***

All of my current possessions were contained in two large suitcases and two boxes in the old summer kitchen of my parents' house. The large box held my bedding and linens, and I had filled the smaller box with books. I had meant to sell more of them but kept taking them off the shelves to keep. Still, there were only a couple dozen volumes, which was a huge reduction.

There was a knock at the door and it opened. David's face appeared. "Somebody call for a moving van?"

"Kind of. Come on in." Amazement registered as he looked at the room which was even more empty than before.

"Wow. Don't have much left, do you?"

"Just enough," I answered, picking up one of the suitcases.

He shook his head. "Wow."

He carried the other suitcase and put them both in the extended cab of the truck. When Dad got home a few minutes later, the two of them loaded my dresser and bed into the back, along with the two boxes. David closed the tailgate.

"You're sure this is it?"

I grinned at him. "One hundred percent sure. I'm traveling light from here on out." I was happy about that and glad to move into the tiny cabin so I'd be around to help Lillian. And this close proximity had to settle once and for all whether David and I had been too much like brother and sister to ever be anything else.

Chapter Twenty-Two

Jim pulled up in his truck and helped David unload the bed and dresser and get them into their new places in the tiny cabin. They left my dresser in the great room, and carefully maneuvered my bed into the sleeping loft, which was accessed by a little set of stairs built into the wall, with storage under each tread. That's where I would put my books and the few dust catchers I kept. There was built-in seating here, including a table that converted to different sizes. At my request, they left the two bags and boxes on the floor of the great room also so I could put everything away myself. I had decided to return Lillian's little love seat because it would feel crowded to have it in the cabin. She had opted to include it in the re-do of her office, which I was glad to hear.

"Gotta run," Jim said, taking a quick look around. "Amazing. Emily, I think you're the only person I know who will rattle around in one hundred and thirty square feet."

"Well, my dad is going to bring my bike and a roller stand. I'm looking forward to riding again, and he and I decided practicing inside was the best way to start."

"Okay, I take back the rattling around part, but you'll still be fine here."

"Better than fine. I really appreciate this little place. It's perfect."

Jim hurried out and drove away in his truck, but David stood on the tiny porch with me and we walked back inside. "You don't ask for much, Emily. I've never known anyone to be so happy with so little."

"I'm much happier now that all the extra stuff is gone. I've done some reading online since I opened my shop, and I guess you would say I've become a minimalist. I kept pieces that really matter to me. The things I love are here." I pointed down at the boxes and didn't make eye contact, because one of them wasn't a thing at all—it was David. Unattainable David who thought of me as a kid sister. That kiss by the river hadn't been repeated. And I knew from the years of finding receipts and notes in his house that he liked women just fine. Perhaps he would never be seriously interested in me or anyone who lived in Serendipity. I thought about it and realized he never had in the past. His weekends were family time, and the weekdays were for work and—play.

I sighed.

"Tired? Is there something else you need from me?"

It took a lot of effort to look into his eyes. "No thanks, David. I'm good. Just need some time to settle in."

His face fell. "Oh—okay. I'll get out of your hair. If Marcus needs any help with the bike and rollers, let me know. As long as it's on the weekend."

Exactly. Because any other time, David wasn't available to me. Not available and not seriously interested. After I watched him drive up the hill, I closed the door and climbed the little staircase to make my bed with fresh sheets and my pretty white comforter. I dropped onto the bed and discovered that if I sat up very straight, I could see David's house from the loft window, even though from downstairs, a hill and some Christmas trees hid it.

I sighed and lay flat, staring at the ceiling. I'd be better off not looking David's direction too often, or I might wish he cared I was so near for some reason other than to be "almost family."

***

"You like living here on the tree farm, don't you, Emily?" Lillian asked one day as we made breakfast together.

"Yes. I love it. I know it's just temporary…."

She held up her hand to stop me. "As far as I'm concerned, the cabin and job are yours as long as you want them. I'm tickled to have you here and to have your help with the bed and breakfast as we build the business."

I went back to scrambling eggs. "So far so good."

She chuckled. "I like the idea of a B&B, but I don't think any of us had given thought to how it would tie me down."

I bit my lip so I wouldn't smile at Lillian's concern about being tied down. She was in her sixties at least and her whole life was in Serendipity.

She washed more fruit for the salad. "Believe it or not, before long I'll start ordering for the Christmas shop. Carla helped me do it online in the past and last year Francie and I managed. But Emily, I do realize if a fulltime job comes along, you will need to do that instead."

I almost hoped the resumes I had sent out wouldn't

yield anything for a while, because I looked forward to working on the tree farm.

Turn the page, Emily.

Ignoring the hallucinatory voice, I said, "It's an honor to help you, Lillian. I mean that. And the tree farm has always been such a special place to me."

"Almost as if there's something magical here?"

I licked my lips, hesitating. "Something like that."

She nodded but didn't say more. I wasn't sure exactly why I'd always had such an attachment to the farm. Certainly, it held a special place in my heart, but the word "magical" hadn't entered my mind.

I was busy every day, helping prepare the cabins for their first occupants and reconfigure the Christmas shop so it could be used as a breakfast area for guests in the off season. And I still cooked dinner with Gran one night a week in her cozy kitchen.

Mom was super busy. Besides managing the new consignment shop, she had converted the old summer kitchen into a staging area for the big party she was going to throw for Hannah and Taylor's high school graduation. Not that I saw them often, but when I did, I noticed subtle changes in the twins' attitudes. They took turns running the shop on Saturdays so Mom could have a day off. They even drove out to see me a few times.

"Perhaps having their own rooms has allowed them to grow up a little bit," Gran suggested one night when I was visiting her. "That's a change you made possible, Emily Elizabeth, by giving up your room."

I shrugged. "That was going to happen eventually."

"But the timing mattered. You made it happen. If you had continued to use the room upstairs while you recuperated, the twins would still be living on top of each other, not able or inclined to find their separate identities. Looking back, I wonder if they might have lashed out because they had the perception that the world was set up as them against everyone else." She sighed. "I'm so glad to see them softening. They really can be quite charming. Instead of using their sense of humor derisively, they just have fun. Well, most of the time anyway. Such a relief."

My BFFs Danielle and Karly and I hung out together as often as we could. I was surprised at how much they liked to come out to the tree farm and sit on my miniature porch to visit.

As summer arrived, more of the cabins were set, and the B&B started to get busy. I loved cleaning the cabins until they sparkled, helping people find their way around the area, and assisting Lillian with breakfast or anything else she wanted me to do.

Simple as my life was, it was more happy and satisfying than ever. I felt as if I was where I was meant to be. Was I being greedy to want David's love on top of all this?

Chapter Twenty-Three

During the conversation weeks ago with Lillian and Gran, I felt as if I had been a pawn in a series of events that benefited Melissa, Jim, and Matthew. But my shop had made a difference in other people's lives and that idea had been mine, not something I'd been thrown into. Matthew's drawing had become part of my business. Melissa's idea for the Christmas tree farm's little cabins had benefited the Standish family but also me. And my having a place of my own was having an effect—positive, I hoped—on my parents' marriage as they got ready to be empty nesters. The pressure Mom and Dad had put on Gran had led to her two apartments, and the ladies there were benefiting from not only a neat place to live but also Gran's wise counsel and friendship.

Gran had said if something is meant to be, it will happen, although circumstances can alter the timing.

And what we do and say affects our family, friends, and sometimes even strangers in ways we may never realize or appreciate.

***

My schedule shifted at David' request, and now I cleaned his house on Saturday mornings. "Gives me a chance to see you instead of having this perception that the place is cleaned by elves once a week," he'd said when asking if I minded the change. It might have been easier on my ego to stay with the old schedule and see David as little as possible, but I didn't want that. Even if we never became more than friends, I enjoyed spending time with him. It was just more heart wrenching than spending time with, say, Karly and Danielle. Plus I didn't want to make a fuss when for the most part, living on the tree farm was ideal for me.

One day when I was cleaning, I ran across the picture I'd given him at *Emily's Dreams*. Good grief— he hadn't done anything with it. I was ready to dump the picture and frame into the trash when he walked in from helping Jim with the trees.

"Hi. Just about to can this. You don't mind, I assume."

He rescued it from my grasp. "Of course I mind. This was my gift from *Emily's Dreams*. It's a keepsake." He looked down at the boy band in its cheap frame. "I can't believe you'd think of canning this."

"Well, if you're so determined to keep it, put a picture in it that you actually want to look at."

"Sure. I just hadn't gotten around to it." He set it onto the counter and took the back off the frame, removed the cardboard backing and the photos inside. The boy band was an item I had cut out of a magazine and put over the picture that had originally been in the frame. What a surprise to see it was an old Christmas photo taken back when the Standish kids were pre-teens. There were Jim and Carla and Francie and David, but David had a baby on his lap. His sisters and brother were doing their fake smiles into the camera, but David was looking at the baby. You could see the baby's face, and its eyes were latched onto David's and a hand wrapped around one of his fingers.

Turn the page, Emily.

I shook my head to clear the voice out of it.

"I don't remember that picture," I said.

"Neither do I." He shrugged. "I'll show this to Mom." He looked up at me, his face inches away. "She invited the two of us for dinner tonight."

I took a moment to catch my breath and straightened to put more distance between us than I wanted to. "That sounds nice."

That evening we walked to her house together.

"Come on in," Lillian invited. "I have vegetable soup on."

"It sounds great. Smells that way too." David winked at me, and we followed Lillian into the kitchen. Her devoted Daisy was standing expectantly at attention.

"Wow, it does smell wonderful, Lillian."

"That's what Daisy thinks. I don't feed her from the table, but Harry did at times." She sighed. "She really was Harry's dog, but she's a great friend to me." She took a plate from near the stove and slid some meat and vegetables into Daisy's dish. The dog immediately gobbled it down.

David laughed. "So you gave Dad grief for feeding her from the table, but you feed her before you even sit down to your own meal?"

She shook a finger at him good-naturedly. "Life changes all of us."

David chuckled and pulled out the picture. "Mom, we found this. I don't remember seeing it before."

Lillian took the photo from him and nodded. "Oh, I remember that day. We have others that are just of the four of you." She led us into the dining room and pointed to a framed photo on the buffet. It certainly was taken the same day. You could tell by the kids' clothes.

Goosebumps had appeared on my arms. I cleared my throat, because although I was almost certain of the answer, I had to ask. "And the baby is...?"

Lillian looked up from the reverie the photo had caused.

"Oh, it's you, of course, Emily. You were just a few months old, and such a mama's girl. Any time someone else tried to hold you, you cried. Even your grandmother." She grinned, shaking her head. "We wanted a photo of all our children together and tried with one of my girls holding you, but your crying kept up. Carla and Francie were nearly in tears because they both thought you were such a cutie and were sure they could get you to settle down. 'Let me do it,' said David. 'She won't cry...will you, Emily?'"

She paused, looking at each of us in turn. "Emily, you stared into his eyes and were mesmerized. When Harry took this photo, everyone was so relieved." She pointed at twelve-year-old Jim, leaning on the arm of the couch ready to run. "Jim looks like he's desperate to be anywhere else." She laughed. "You never did cry as long as David held you. It was amazing. Reba and I agreed that day there was a special connection between the two of you. And look how it has turned out."

I stared at the photo, touched by her story.

"Mom, you sound like a matchmaker."

She shrugged, and her eyes twinkled. "Nothing of the sort, David. We know better than to meddle in people's lives. Certainly Reba or I might make the occasional suggestion...."

I remembered the many times Gran had *suggested* a boyfriend of mine wasn't right for me. Not that she necessarily did it in words but usually with a look, because with Gran, that's often all that was required.

David put his arm around Lillian's slender shoulders. "You might just as well come clean. Admit that for Emily's entire life, you've been setting us up." He didn't look all that upset about it.

Lillian shook her head. "David, you know I've done nothing of the sort, and neither has Reba." She reached out and took my hands, leaned into David. "If Reba and I had been matchmaking, we could have saved a lot of time for everyone, but events have to unfold on their own. You both had to find your own way." She sighed. "Just thinking of all the twists and turns and heartache makes me absolutely famished. Let's have some of the soup before Daisy helps herself to the rest of it."

At least two people seemed to know exactly where

David and I were heading. Unfortunately, those two people weren't David and me—they were my grandmother and his mom.

Chapter Twenty-Four

"How does that make you feel, Emily?" We were walking from Lillian's down the path to my cabin. "The fact that my mom and your grandmother had this premonition about us?"

"I don't know. Confused? I've had so many relationships that ended badly." What I wanted was for David to give me some reassurance about his thoughts of the future.

"Confused is a good word. And I've definitely had a lot of relationships. Nothing long-term, ever. And nothing serious." He took a giant step ahead and stopped, facing me. "You know why?"

Dying to know. "Um. Nope. Why?"

"I was waiting for you."

I laughed out loud before I could stop myself.

"Don't laugh at me. You may not have thought of me that way, but all my life, I've tried to look out for you. At first, it was because you didn't have a big brother to do it and you were sort of wildly independent. Well, it turned out you didn't need me to look out for you. Look at all you've done."

"Me? What have I done?"

"You're kidding. You came back from that car wreck, kicked into gear at rehab, and when you got out, you started getting rid of the past you weren't happy with. I've never seen anybody so determined to change their life. And in changing your life, you've helped a lot of people. My mom, your mom, your sisters, lots of people who made purchases and were given extras at your shop. Who knows how much good you've done or set into motion?"

He took my hand. "All your life, I've been just plain old boring David, but I was dependable. I gave you your first job and no matter what else transpired in your life, the job was there. I was around, if you'd wanted me when you got old enough, but you didn't. And that had to be okay with me, if I was just interested in what was best for you." His eyes grew brighter. "But now, I hope you see I'm not quite as boring, or as ancient, as you thought. You know, you didn't need to change yourself in order to start your new life. You needed to change the way you saw things—and people."

His voice dropped to a whisper. "So, now you're seeing things differently, see this—the face of the man who loves you and always has."

"Oh, David." I was suddenly in his arms, cradled like that little baby for a moment and then kissed until I thought I'd died and gone to heaven after all.

Chapter Twenty-Five

Kim Rose and I sat on my tiny porch drinking lemonade.

"This is the most peaceful place I've ever been." She leaned back against a wall, closed her eyes and sighed.

"Same here. I've always loved the tree farm."

"And you're going to invite me to that wedding, right?"

"I didn't say anything about a wedding."

"Princess, you don't have to spell everything out for me. I see it on your face, and I could hear it in your voice on the phone. Good old David-just-a-friend-of-the-family has turned into something more." She sighed. "All in good time."

"Okay, yes. We're—getting serious. The word 'wedding' hasn't come up yet, but I have an idea it won't be long. I'd love to get married right here on the tree farm."

She opened her eyes and sat up. "That would be gorgeous, Princess. You and your tiara and white dress and the knight rides up on his horse—just kidding. You know I'm happy for you."

"I'm so happy with David and so happy living here and helping Lillian. But I keep waiting to figure out what it is my life is supposed to turn into."

She looked at me blankly. "Huh?"

"You know. You're working toward becoming a nurse because of being sick. Well, I don't have a focus like that. I don't have the inclination to become a nurse or a physical therapist. I mean, those are awesome careers, and I'm super thankful for the people who helped me. but I don't think I'm cut out for it."

"Yeah. Not everybody is. Otherwise, there wouldn't be any jobs at all."

"So, what then? I'm twenty-five with no college degree and no direction in life."

"Gee, Emily, how awful for you. You're living in the Garden of Eden, in love with a dreamy guy who's loved you forever, and there's no evil serpent in sight."

"Sure, life is great, but what—"

"Princess, surely you don't think you have to go to college to make a difference in this world."

"Well…."

"You've made a huge difference in your little town from what I understand. Hey, I stopped in Serendipity to use the bathroom at the gas station, and when I told the girl with the key who I was going to visit, she couldn't sing your praises long or loud enough. People here seem to think pretty highly of you. Emily Kincaid, the girl who survived a near-fatal wreck, worked hard to get her body to heal, and when she got home she was all about making other people's lives better. These things you gave people? I mean, not sold, but gave— ooh—gives me shivers to think of the stories they told me."

"They?"

"The girl with the bathroom key and the guy who was buying coffee. And, well, a couple of other people who were buying stuff, and the boyfriend of the girl with the bathroom key. I think he was just hanging out." She waved them away. "But what I'm saying is that you, Princess, have done a lot of good in this little town since you came here from Meadowbrooke. Pretty cool stuff, and I can say I knew you when." She sipped her lemonade and leaned back against the house. "Now let's talk wedding colors. No need to ruin a perfectly beautiful day living in the past."

Chapter Twenty-Six

After so many months of not having the opportunity, or being physically able, there was finally an evening when Melissa and Jim wanted to go on a date and Lillian wasn't able to babysit. I was happy to take care of Matthew, and he asked if he could spend the night with me instead of me coming to their big house on North Main Street for a few hours.

"You're sure you don't mind, Emily?" Melissa asked. "It seems such an imposition."

"I'd love it, Melissa. My first official sleepover."

It was a weeknight, so David was on the road. I'd talked to him earlier than usual, so I could focus on Matthew when he arrived.

I happily made up a bed for him next to mine in the loft. He loved the idea of sleeping up there and had been up and down the stairs a dozen times during the evening. He was more than ready to call it a night when I told him it was bedtime. First, I read the new book I'd bought for him that featured a dog that resembled Lillian's sweet Daisy. When I set it aside, I opened one of my childhood favorites, a book of poems and rhymes. We skipped a lot of the poems that had pictures of girls next to them because Matthew didn't want to hear about "girl stuff."

I stopped at the page containing my favorite picture in the book and the poem *Afternoon on a Hill*, by Edna St. Vincent Millay. Suddenly my mind was full of the day I had awakened from a dream of *being* the blond girl on the hill of daisies. That day I had been at the point of death. I looked at the girl in the picture, whose hair was being blown back from her face by the breeze. She was staring resolutely into the wind, but the picture doesn't show what she's looking at.

After a few moments I recovered and was able to read the poem to Matthew, thinking he probably wouldn't get much out of it, but hey—you keep feeding a child culture and maybe it eventually clicks. When I finished the poem, I noticed he was studying the page.

"What are you thinking about, Matthew? Do you like that poem?"

He shrugged. "The girl is sad a long time."

"Why do you say that?"

"She has a sad face. The wind talks, but she won't listen."

Well, that was imaginative. *The wind talks.* "Okay. What do you think the wind is telling her?"

"The wind says 'Don't be in the field.'" His voice was solemn.

"And…where is she supposed to be?"

"Em'ly! She's s'posed to be in the trees!" He looked at me as if that should be obvious. "In the Christmas trees."

"Oh, Matthew. That's nice to think, because you love this Christmas tree farm. It is a special place, but just because we like it a lot, doesn't mean that's where we *belong*, does it?" I thought I should try to be a little realistic, after all.

Matthew shook his head, unimpressed by my attempt to get back to reality. "The girl is s'posed to be in the trees! Turn the page, Em'ly!"

"I—what?"

"Turn the page, Emily."

I had heard that sentence many times in the last few months. But this time, it was finally a voice I knew.

It was Matthew Singer's voice, matter-of-factly asking to see the next page of a favorite book from my childhood. My hand shouldn't have been shaking as I reached up to do as he asked.

A snowy scene covered the two-page spread, hills of evergreens, and a single-story house tucked snugly into a hill with smoke cheerfully puffing out the chimney. My eyes blurred with sudden tears as I recognized the painting's uncanny similarity to the Standish tree farm and David's house. Although it was familiar, I hadn't particularly remembered this picture from previous readings of the book, and right now my teary eyes couldn't focus on whatever poem was printed below it.

"See?" Matthew pointed at the house. "She goes there, Em'ly. She goes to that house." He beamed up at me. "The path is steep, but she is strong enough to do it. Right?"

"Yes," I whispered. "Yes, I think that's exactly right."

Matthew took the book and closed it gently and held it on his lap as he snuggled more into my embrace. "Now the girl is all done being sad." He patted my hand and sighed.

***

I never again heard a mysterious voice telling me to *turn the page*. And I never looked at a daisy the same way I had before. Instead of just being a pretty, happy flower, daisies became for me a symbol of starting over. Because it was when I was the girl sitting in the field of daisies that I somehow chose to start my life over and go, at last, in the right direction.

At first, my progress had been slow—my body and my soul had to heal and my outlook had to change and broaden before I could get to that next page. But when the time was right, what joy I found on the page of my life with the beautiful Christmas tree farm and the man who lived there. I had loved them for twenty-five years so far and would continue to do so forever.

The End...or is it The Beginning?

From the Author

I hope you've enjoyed reading *Emily's Dreams*. When I started writing the story at the request of readers of *Small Town Christmas*, I wasn't sure what Emily's journey to wholeness would be. As usual, not plotting the story ahead of time offered both challenges and opportunities. Emily was slow to reveal what was going on with her, but when she finally did, I realized her journey could be worthwhile for many readers.

How many of us have wished for an opportunity to start over, yet when the chance came along, fell back into old habits instead of trying something new? Emily is here to tell us that stepping into the unknown is not only possible, but has its own rewards. Following one's heart may upset a status quo, but perhaps that isn't as unsettling for onlookers as we might expect. Perhaps, in fact, the onlookers are watching for pointers so they can step out themselves.

Isn't it nice to think that, just like Emily, each of us has an important contribution to make in this world?

Magdalena Scott

Please visit my website to sign up for my newsletter, contact me by email, read about my Serendipity and Legend series books, and connect via social media.

www.magdalenascott.com

Also in the Serendipity, Indiana, series:

Small Town Christmas

Melissa is moving back to Serendipity, Indiana to raise her young son and run her new business—in spite of a painful past and the fact that her ex-boyfriend still lives in their hometown.

Coming in Autumn 2015:

Christmas Wedding

Dec. 1: Jim Standish is ready—right this minute—to marry the love of his life, but Melissa Singer wants the day to be one they'll look back on forever. Planning and execution time: 25 days. Will it be possible to create the perfect Christmas Wedding?

Future Serendipity Titles:

The Blank Book

Alice Williams is surviving widowhood, but must unlock the secrets of a mysterious blank book before she can confidently step into her future with a man she's afraid to love.

The Road not Taken

Francie Standish Carrington has some tough decisions to make, and a lot of questions about a past she thought she understood.

The Ring

A fascinating man has stepped into Carla Standish's perfect life. He's brought a beautiful gift, lots of baggage, and a promise he may not be able to fulfill.

A Piece of Her Soul

Jacqueline needs a break from the constant strain of the special gift she has. But the little cottage on a quiet street isn't quite the retreat she expected, due to the presence of a handsome next door neighbor.

Magdalena's Legend, Tennessee Titles

Midnight in Legend, TN

Christmas Collision

Where Her Heart Is

Building a Dream

Under the Mistletoe

The Holly and the Ivy

Second Chances